"I'm Not Looking For Trouble...."

"Then why did you come back to this one-horse town when you know you ain't exactly the favorite hometown boy?" the bartender asked Leander.

The door opened as if in answer, and the bartender said, "Will you get a load of what the storm just blew in? It's your wife."

Leander turned and froze. He felt as if he'd been hit by a cyclone. She looked sexy...and scared.

"You want to hear the joke of the century? I came back because of her."

"Then you were damn sure lying when you said you weren't looking for trouble, 'cause that's all that rich debutante has ever been for you."

"So what else is new? Merry Christmas." Leander took a pill from the bottle. "I was born on Christmas Eve. Did anybody ever tell you that? Same night she was. She used to say that meant she was my destiny. What kind of crazy sucker would fall for a line like that?"

Reflections from the Christmas lights gleamed in the bartender's eyes.

"You tell me—sucker."

Dear Reader,

As a very special treat this season, Silhouette Desire is bringing you the best in holiday stories. It's our gift from us—the editorial staff at Silhouette—to you, the readers. The month begins with a very special MAN OF THE MONTH from Ann Major, *A Cowboy Christmas*. Years ago, a boy and girl were both born under the same Christmas star. She grew up rich; he grew up poor…and when they met, they fell into a love that would last a lifetime….

Next, Anne McAllister's CODE OF THE WEST series continues with *Cowboys Don't Stay*, the third book in her series about the Tanner brothers.

Christmas weddings are always a lot of fun, and that's why we're bringing you *Christmas Wedding* by Pamela Macaluso. And if Texas is a place you'd like to spend the holidays—along with a sexy Texas man—don't miss *Texas Pride* by Barbara McCauley. Next, popular Silhouette Romance writer Sandra Steffen makes her Desire debut with *Gift Wrapped Dad*.

Finally, do not miss *Miracles and Mistletoe,* another compelling love story from the talented pen of Cait London.

So, from our "house" to yours…Happy Holidays.

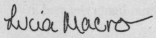

Lucia Macro

Please address questions and book requests to:
Silhouette Reader Service
U.S.: 3010 Walden Ave., P.O. Box 1325, Buffalo, NY 14269
Canadian: P.O. Box 609, Fort Erie, Ont. L2A 5X3

Ann Major

A COWBOY CHRISTMAS

SILHOUETTE *Desire*®
Published by Silhouette Books
America's Publisher of Contemporary Romance

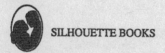

SILHOUETTE BOOKS

ISBN 0-373-05967-1

A COWBOY CHRISTMAS

Copyright © 1995 by Ann Major

Printed in U.S.A.

Books by Ann Major

Silhouette Desire

Dream Come True #16
Meant To Be #35
Love Me Again #99
The Wrong Man #151
Golden Man #198
Beyond Love #229
In Every Stranger's Face #301
What This Passion Means #331
*Passion's Child #445
*Destiny's Child #451
*Night Child #457
*Wilderness Child #535
*Scandal's Child #564
*The Goodbye Child #648
A Knight in Tarnished Armor #690
Married to the Enemy #716
†Wild Honey #805
†Wild Midnight #819
†Wild Innocence #835
The Accidental Bridegroom #889
A Cowboy Christmas #967

*Children of Destiny series
†Something Wild

Silhouette Special Edition

Brand of Diamonds #83
Dazzle #229
The Fairy Tale Girl #390

Silhouette Intimate Moments

Seize the Moment #54

Silhouette Romance

Wild Lady #90
A Touch of Fire #150

Silhouette Books

Silhouette Christmas Stories 1990
"Santa's Special Miracle"

Silhouette Summer Sizzlers 1992
"The Barefooted Enchantress"

Birds, Bees and Babies 1994
"The Baby Machine"

Silhouette Summer Sizzlers 1995
"Fancy's Man"

ANN MAJOR

loves writing romance novels as much as she loves reading them. She is the proud mother of three children who are now in high school and college. She lists hiking in the Colorado mountains with her husband, playing tennis, sailing, enjoying her cats and playing the piano among her favorite activities.

Prologue

The Dairy Princess, which served better gossip than hamburgers, never lacked for a crowd. That particular Christmas in Kinney, Texas, the hottest flavor on the DP menu was once again the latest development in the star-crossed romance of the local rich girl and the town's favorite bad boy cowboy.

"Did you hear that Leander Knight won Heddy Kinney in a game of five-card stud?"

An expectant hush fell over the DP.

"No!"

"And her supposed to marry that millionaire—"

"Well, she up and ran off to Mexico with Pepper—on her wedding night!" "Pepper" was the townsfolk's nickname for Leander.

As one-horse towns go in south Texas, Kinney was pretty dull. It had a rusty water tower that could be seen from the highway. It had a grocery store, a hardware store, a gas station, the Dairy Princess and two very disreputable bars.

Other than the fabled comings and goings at the big Kinney Ranch, there never was much to talk about. So, when Jim Bob Janovich phoned his mother on Christmas Eve from the French Quarter to say that Pepper had shown up drunk in the bar of the hotel where Heddy and her famous groom were about to take up honeymooning and had taunted the bridegroom into a card game while the bride was upstairs sprucing herself up for the big night, everybody got mighty interested. Especially after Jim Bob said Pepper had won her.

"Pepper always was a wild one."

"He was wild about Heddy, if that's what you mean," Flora Janovich said.

"You'd better worry about Old Man Kinney putting a bullet right between Pepper's pretty black eyes."

"No chance of that," someone else said. "I hear Heddy and Pepper hightailed it to Mexico."

The telephone lines buzzed. When the Kinneys returned New Year's Eve in a snit without Heddy, neither Barret, Heddy's father, who was usually a jovial fellow, but who'd been behaving mighty erratically of late, nor Tia, her imperious grandmother, would talk to a soul or show their faces in town.

So, without so much as a morsel of fresh gossip to chew on that week, all a curious body could do was rehash the old story that they all knew by heart about how Leander Knight and Heddy Kinney had got started in the first place.

They'd been born the same hour, under that same too-bright star, on that same Christmas Eve in Kinney, but nobody would have ever thought of matching them up then. For the golden-haired girl's birth had been looked forward to by her proud family, who were members of the local ranching aristocracy. Her birth was feted and written about even though her father, Barret Kinney, would have preferred a son.

The little boy, born less than a minute after she, was found half-dead in a garbage Dumpster by a wino who'd crawled inside to get warm that Christmas Day. Black-haired, black-eyed, swarthy-skinned, the infant was swaddled in a plastic garbage sack and rushed to the same hospital and laid beside her crib in the brightly lit, warm nursery. He began to kick the instant he was fed, his vulgar energy upstaging the pale little princess beside him and amazing and disgusting her family when they came to bestow their gifts of admiration upon her. But an old nurse, who loved both babies, would rock them together after all Heddy's fancy visitors had gone, and she told everybody who would listen that when Heddy was taken to her mother to nurse, the boy fretted till she was brought back and placed beside him in his crib.

Heddy was dressed in imported lace and taken home to a huge mansion decked in holly and ivy. The house sat on a low hill on her father's legendary ranch. There she was adored and petted, especially by her grandmother. Her family wanted only the best for her. Beneath their tall Christmas tree in the center of the ballroom, her gifts that had not been opened were piled high for her. Two hundred guests attended her christening the next month.

He was bounced from one shabby foster home to the next.

When her mother died the next year, and the little girl grew into a tomboy who preferred to run wild and free with her father and the vaqueros, Tia, her strong-willed grandmother, began to worry. For Tia, whose husband had recently died in a New Orleans hospital of a mysterious illness, had grand plans for her baby princess.

From their two separate worlds, these children came. They were ten years old when they met at school and were instantly attracted. He had suffered shame and loneliness and grown tough. Having lost her own mother, Heddy was drawn to Pepper, who had lost both parents.

He had just been adopted by the Widow Janovich, and it was his first day at school. Since she was a Kinney, she was the most admired child in their school. The bullies had knocked him and Jim Bob to the ground and were chanting at him, "Bastard! We don't like you! We won't play with you! Not ever!"

Heddy pushed through them. Two boys lay on the ground hemmed in by the hostile throng—the bigger of the pair, Jim Bob Janovich was red-faced and blubbering. But the center of attention was the slim boy lying in the dirt who hadn't given up the fight. When Tom Yates tackled him from behind, he fought back, rolling on the pavement, clawing and kicking like a wildcat until five more jumped him.

"Stop it!" she screamed.

The bullies scowled at her, but she scowled harder. Until finally, with blood trickling from their mouths, they slunk several feet away, leaving the stranger lying on the ground alone.

When she knelt closer he glared up at her, his insolent black eyes burning with a fierce animal excitement that sickened her. He was skinny, yet he was the most magnificently fearsome boy she had ever seen. For a long moment she studied his torn clothes, his dark sullen face that was somehow so incredibly attractive despite its bruises and cuts and that terrifying wildness that was so much a part of him.

She spun on her silent classmates. "You leave him alone. I'll play with him."

As if by magic his tormentors vanished. Not that the new boy showed any gratitude as she led him to a water fountain where she cleaned him up and told him he wouldn't look nearly as awful if he'd smile and say a thank-you.

"Who made you queen of the world?"

"I did," Heddy replied with a pert smile. "And my grandmother, Tía."

"So—does everybody always do what you say?"

"Mostly."

"Not me. I don't do what anybody says."

Her chin went up a notch. "We'll see."

He picked up a rock and threw it defiantly so that it arced high over the seesaws into the piercing blue sky.

She picked up one and threw it, and it sailed just as far. "I can catch fireflies, dozens of them, with my bare hands and not hurt them. I've got a pet snake and a pony I can ride better than any of the vaqueros. I can—"

"Who cares? What are you trying to prove with all your braggin', girl?"

"Same thing you are—that I'm just like everybody else."

"But you're not," he said. "You're different—like me. I'm all alone. I don't need anybody. And you're queen of the town."

"But I feel all alone, too."

She had looked into his dark eyes and been startled to find her own soul mirrored there.

When Heddy found out they shared the same birthday, she said, "That means our destiny's the same, too."

"That's silly."

They had become instant best friends, a relationship her snobbish family considered undesirable. Especially when he grew more handsome as time passed and more acceptable to the other kids in their class. Especially when, except for the occasional lapses of youthful wildness, his career through school was amazingly honorable. When he wasn't studying or playing football, he worked to help Mrs. Janovich. He had a way with words and was always winning writing contests.

Every Christmas Eve, Leander always found Heddy and said, "Happy birthday. Merry Christmas." Then they exchanged presents.

Not that their relationship was perfectly harmonious. She was outgoing while he was a loner. She was rich and headstrong and spoiled. He was sometimes defensive about his low position in the town compared to hers. Occasionally he got angry at her or her family for their imagined or real high-handed treatment of him.

But they were always so miserable when they quarreled that they made up quickly.

Eight years later, when Heddy's family sent her away to college and she made her debut in New Orleans, the Kinneys thought they had separated her forever from the cowboy who didn't have a cent to call his own and probably never would. Though they never said so, they thought he lacked everything that mattered most to them in a prospective son-in-law—breeding, moneyed connections and land. The fact that Heddy and he were soul mates and star siblings did not matter in the Kinneys' wealthy world of privilege. Nor did they wish to gamble on his innate talent and intelligence. They weren't impressed when he sold his very first short stories to good magazines. They believed writers were a starving, unpredictable breed and that their Heddy would be happier and safer with her own kind.

They thought she would realize that rich girls didn't marry poor boys like Leander Knight.

But in that they misjudged her....

Intermittent bursts of lightning lit the shimmering wet black windowpanes. Standing by the window, with her gleaming hair and violet blue eyes, Heddy was a vision of golden loveliness in her gossamer nightgown.

It was her wedding night, and her bridegroom had abandoned her. Most girls would have been devastated; Heddy Kinney was drinking champagne and enjoying the thunderstorm.

The New Orleans newspapers had called it the wedding of the century. They had described the groom's thirty-room mansion, his twenty-two polo ponies, with immense enthusiasm. Her ranch had been photographed with equal attention. She and Bronier DuChamp had stood arm in arm, staring at each other adoringly in countless pictures...at countless parties. As if being beautiful and rich and having lots of great stuff really meant they were the perfect couple.

Ha!

What would everybody think if they found out the lonely bride was getting herself thoroughly tipsy?

Some wedding night!

But so far it was better than she'd expected.

The champagne caught the light from the lamps as Heddy swiveled the crystal stem of her glass between her fingers. Her creamy skin glowed.

She wondered if Bro was ever coming.

Worse, she wondered if she even cared.

Heddy's travel alarm clock ticked steadily as she tipped her champagne flute to her lips. She'd been listening to the little black clock for over an hour—ever since Bro had misinterpreted her dread for shyness and offered to go down to the bar and have a drink with his best man while she got ready.

She went to the champagne bucket, pulled the bottle from the ice and poured herself another glassful. She wondered suddenly if he loved her, or if he was as scared as she was, if her marriage was doomed, as all her relationships had been since she'd left Kinney . . . and . . . Leander.

Outside in the Quarter, the rain drummed fiercely.

Last night had been beautiful and balmy.

Last night she had walked in the silvery moonlight with another man. She frowned slightly. She couldn't let herself think of that.

Instead she concentrated on the storm and the ticking clock. When she went to the window to watch the rain again, the night chill seeping through the windows made her shiver.

She heard the elevator bell, then a man's stumbling steps in the hall, his mumbled curses when he dropped something on the carpet—maybe his key.

When he fell against the door and then turned his key in the lock, she tensed.

Pretend you love him. Maybe someday you will.

She'd played the pretend game all this past year. Ever since that awful night when Jim Bob had called and told her that Leander had left her for a new girl.

No matter that Leander had shown up last night at the rehearsal dinner, swearing there had never been another girl, that he had only asked Jim Bob to call to make it easier for her to forget him and live the high life her family wanted her to.

He'd been passionately sweet, coaxing her out for a moonlit walk where she'd melted into his arms. One kiss, and he'd begged her to run away with him, swearing he'd been so lonely without her he'd nearly died. One kiss, and she might have gone if Bronier and Tia hadn't found her, and she'd recovered her senses.

The door swung open as Heddy took another gulp of champagne. It tasted warm and flat, and she felt a vague nausea as she smoothed her hair.

Instead of racing toward the door, she set her glass down.

Which was a mistake.

Because it was Leander, not Bro, who staggered inside. Leander, looking rougher and more unkempt, wilder and angrier and yet somehow more unsure of himself than she'd ever seen him. Leander, whose hot, insolent black eyes sent a paralyzing shaft of fear darting through her.

Other than her hand going to her throat, she remained motionless. Which gave him the precious seconds he needed to bolt the door and jam the key deep inside his tight jeans.

Dressed in the same black T-shirt and scuffed boots as last night, his expression was icily dangerous. There were smudges of exhaustion under his eyes, and black stubble shadowing his jaw.

His shoulders were wide; his biceps bulged. His wavy, coal black hair was uncombed and falling across his dark brow.

Her skin was bathed and scented; her long hair had been brushed a hundred times; her nails polished pearl pink. She was as meticulously groomed as he was uncouth.

"Howdy, Sugar," he drawled in a measured voice that told her he'd had too much to drink. He took off his hat, bowed in a mockingly respectful gesture and pitched it toward the nearest gilt chair. It sailed across the antique sofa and landed on a plump pillow of her magnificent bed.

"Oops." He grinned at her and stumbled forward. "And happy birthday, and Merry Christmas and all that rot—"

Their old greeting. And yet it wasn't.

He held out two wrapped boxes.

"What are you doing here?" she whispered, aware suddenly that at the mere sight of him, angry and liquored-up though he was, her body had caught dangerously on fire.

When his devil black eyes went over her and lit with a fire of their own, she realized that her negligee and peignoir were so transparent she might as well be nude.

"This is my wedding night," she whispered, grabbing a blanket to cover herself.

"*Was* your wedding night, Sugar." His slurred, sexy voice was ice. "Don't remind me."

"You have no right."

He tossed his presents toward a low table and fanned four crumpled playing cards in her face proudly. "I won you, Sugar. Not fair and square. First time I ever cheated." He flipped the cards into the air. "Check out the winning hand!"

Not knowing what he was talking about, she stared as four cards, a pair of two's and a pair of three's, fell onto the carpet. "What did you do to Bro? Why isn't he here?"

"Your precious bridegroom can't hold his liquor. He's not much of a card player, either. He drank himself into a stupor after he lost you to such a lousy hand. I left him in the bar sprawled on the floor, holding a pair of jacks."

When Leander grinned cockily, she swayed toward him. "You bastard..."

"Now, go easy, Sugar." His gentle purr was savage now. "You know how I prefer *orphan* or *adopted* or some politically correct piece of garbage like *disadvantaged by birth.*"

When she lunged at him, he staggered backward against the wall. He grinned as he caught her wrists and hauled her into his arms. Then he glimpsed her wedding rings, and his smile died.

The circlets of platinum suddenly felt as cold as ice burning her finger. His narrow, hooded eyes pierced her soul. He held her firmly, yet he was careful not to hurt her.

Close up, his face was lean and hard, his carved features possessing a dangerous beauty that left her breathless. Close up he reeked of cheap liquor and sweat. But she didn't care.

"I wanted to put you out of my mind forever, Sugar. I hated always being told I wasn't good enough."

"I—I never—"

"Not you, baby. But everybody else in town thought you were grand and I was dirt. Especially Tia." His expression darkened. "I tried to forget you. I tried again last night after you left me for Bro. Then I watched you together."

His roughly callused hands were entangled in her golden hair, jerking her head back. "You looked so unhappy in his arms. I kept thinking how you lit up when you first saw me last night. How maybe your know-it-all family didn't know what was best for you after all. I went to a bar and damn near drank myself to death, but, drunk or sober, all I saw was your face. I couldn't live with the thought of you being unhappy."

Her pulses were beating heavily as he lowered his mouth to hers. "So, Sugar, is it really over between us?"

"Yes."

Then why was her voice so raspy and soft? Why couldn't she breathe? Why was her body tense with expectation because his mouth was so near?

"Or do you still have the hots for me?"

"Are you crazy? You smell like a brewery!"

"Sorry about that, Sugar. No toothbrush. Guess I'll have to borrow yours—" He dragged her toward the bathroom.

She should have slapped him or tried to run. But her body burned, and her heart ached.

He was spraying water everywhere when she turned the faucet off and took her toothbrush from him.

He turned back to her. She was tense and still. When he saw the hunger in her eyes, his voice softened. "I love you, Sugar."

Those four velvet words resonated in her soul.

She didn't move as his mouth met hers. His hands slid over her, molding her slender curves to his hard flesh.

"I've always loved you," he said as the warmth of his body engulfed hers. "I always will."

Then her heart began to beat violently.

She didn't know whether he was taking her to heaven or to hell—but she didn't care. She wanted his mouth on her lips again, his mouth all over her body.

Slowly he kissed her, a long, soft, undemanding kiss. But it seemed to her that the world shook and that he was the only solid thing she could cling to. And she knew that if his single drunken kiss could ignite such blazing need, her grand marriage to Bronier was a travesty.

When Leander picked her up to carry her to the bed, her arms wound eagerly around his neck. Her family, especially Tia, would do everything in their power to destroy them. But she didn't care. Tomorrow she would go down on her knees and beg Bro's forgiveness when she told him she couldn't be his wife because no matter how she had tried to pretend otherwise, she had always belonged to Leander.

Slowly she took off her engagement ring and her wedding band and laid them on the nightstand.

"Merry Christmas," she said as she'd said so many times during their childhood when they'd secretly exchanged forbidden presents. "Happy birthday." Her throat tightened. "I'm sorry I don't have presents for you."

There was an enigmatic darkness to his eyes. "Oh, but you do." He slid her peignoir from her shoulders and cupped her breasts. "You're about to give me the best presents I ever had."

"How do you know? You haven't unwrapped them yet."

"Ah, Heddy," she heard him say right before he pulled her under him. "You were always so sweet to me when we were kids. You could be a royal pain, too. But nobody was ever as sweet."

She fumbled urgently with his shirt, pushing it over his head, needing to feel his bare skin under her hands. He did not resist when she eagerly splayed her fingers through the crisp, black hair that matted his chest and then ran her hands downward, exploring the virile muscled contours of his body.

He felt so good. So perfect. With every passing moment, she grew hotter for him. She wished he would hurry, that his fingers and mouth would touch her more intimately. That he would take her fast and hard. And then make love to her again very slowly.

He smiled at her, laughing softly, pulling away a little, now that he knew she was as eager as he.

He began ripping at the snaps of his jeans, sliding them down, hopping on one foot, then the other to get out of them as he backed away from the bed.

"Hey, where are you going?"

"To take a shower. To brush my teeth."

"No—"

"Sugar, I slept in a storm sewer last night with three homeless guys that didn't smell too good."

She lay in bed, feeling lonely and restless while he showered.

He returned almost instantly, his black hair wet and shining as he lay down beside her. His minty-tasting mouth sought her lips, his tongue sliding inside.

"The first time I saw you, it was as if I already knew you," he said a long time later. "As if I'd lived somewhere in some other time or planet with you. As if you had always been a part of me and always would be."

She ran a fingertip down the length of his nose, liking the way he shuddered even from her light touch. "I felt the same way. But my family—"

He slid his hand under the straps of her nightgown. "What can they do, if we love each other?"

He pushed her nightgown lower and kissed each nipple. Her gown was only halfway off when she began arching her body against his and moaning his name. Sensing her need, he didn't bother to undress her. Ripping the sheets back, he lifted her gown above her thighs, searching out the hot damp sweetness between her legs. When she felt his hand there, she inhaled sharply. Then he was lowering his body to hers, and she was urging him inside her, her arms gripping him fiercely. When he thrust forward, ripples of pleasure convulsed through every part of her.

His heart pounded like thunder.

It had been too long for them both.

He moved once, and they exploded.

"Sorry, Sugar," he murmured, burying his face against her cheek.

She wrapped her arms around him, clinging to him, drawing him closer as he began to make love to her again.

She kissed his damp brow, ran her hand through his wet hair. He was everything. She loved him, and she was sure that her family, even Tia, would love him too once they realized what he meant to her.

Two weeks later, after her marriage had been annulled and she'd legally married Leander in Mexico, they went home to Kinney.

Shortly after that the trouble started.

Within a year, Leander was one of the richest and most famous horror novelists in the world.

But his marriage was over.

And he had an unsavory, if undeserved reputation.

It was a widely known fact that Barret Kinney thought Leander Knight had married his daughter for their ranch and that Barret hated him and berated him constantly. Thus, when Barret was found shot in the head after a quarrel with Leander, Leander was suspected of murder. Then Tia suffered a heart attack shortly afterward, and Leander was blamed for that, too.

Not that there had been a shred of evidence against Leander.

Not that he was ever formally charged.

Not that Tia, who hated him, or Heddy, who loved him, ever said a word in public against him.

The gossips tried him, found him guilty, and damned him.

But it was Heddy's coldness that drove him out of town.

Alone in New York, Leander wrote his first novel, *Dead Ringer*—to exonerate himself.

Leander hated the sordid publicity surrounding his book, but it made him one of the hottest names in the publishing world. The journalistic slant was that he was a creepy killer who murdered his famous, wealthy father-in-law and wrote a novel about it to get rich.

He hadn't written the book to bring more scandal on the Kinney family. Nor to drive Heddy and his baby daughter even further away. Nor to make everybody in Kinney resent him even more. But that was what happened.

His fame soon grew to international proportions. Every time a new Leander Knight title hit the stands, the media rehashed the sordid story, magnifying the horror of Barret's mysterious death and implicating Leander as a gold digger and a murderer, as an opportunist who'd reaped fame and fortune after marrying into and then destroying one of the most famous families in Texas. Leander's early novels were reissued, especially the first. Nobody noticed that in his first novel, the hero had been framed.

The more successful Leander became, the more scary the media made him out to be. In the beginning Leander granted interviews in a naive attempt to clear his name. But his words were always twisted against him. The photographs of him that appeared in magazines were darkened to make him look more macabre.

In the end he grew so fed up with all the lies that he moved to a remote island in southern Alaska. And because it was impossible to hound anyone if he chose to flee to an uninhabitable winter wilderness where unpaved roads and ports were cut off by glaciers and snowstorms and mountains, where the few existing airstrips were fogged in by low clouds for weeks at a time, he escaped them.

For eight years Leander lived simply in Alaska and produced two megabestsellers a year, each outselling the one before. Each adding to his notoriety and his unsavory reputation as a killer-writer. Each widening the chasm between himself and his wife and daughter. He was at the top of bestseller lists all over the world. He reached the fantasy level of success that all writers dream about.

But he despised his fame. Because it had cost him his family and his reputation.

As for the writing—it was simply something he had to do. He would have done it for nothing. But it was a lonely occupation, and he was a lonely man. He was afraid to drink because liquor loosened his inner control and made his loneliness dangerously unbearable. Halfway through a bottle something inside him would break and he would feel a desperate, long-buried yearning for Texas and the golden-haired woman he had loved and lost. For Christina, their daughter, who had grown up without him.

He would have exchanged all his millions for an honorable life with the two of them.

One
***

The winter weather on the Alaskan island had been clear for a couple of hours around noon yesterday, so Leander knew the weekly mail plane from Juneau had probably been able to get to the village. He had a large house in Juneau, a computer, a secretary and a research assistant. Nevertheless, he preferred the isolation of his tiny cabin on the island and still spent as much time as possible there.

He came down by snowmobile, attentive to the familiar landmarks in the morning's dim winter light as he carefully approached the outskirts of the remote village which was a mere half hour upriver from his cabin even in bad conditions. Ivak, his Alaskan husky, loped happily behind him on the ice.

Usually Leander worked in his cabin till late afternoon. But his novel in progress had him stumped. He was nearly finished, and way before his deadline, but the ending lacked sizzle. There was no do-or-die climactic moment of choice for the hero, so that the reader could see what his character was made of and what his monster was made of. Leander had grown bored with his supernatural homicidal maniac, and he was afraid his readers would be just as bored if he didn't think up a new twist in the plot. So, he'd decided to break early and let his subconscious mind mull on the problem.

The icy wind slashed at him as the snowmobile flew over the snow. He welcomed the bracing cold; he welcomed the danger of it, the challenge, even as he looked forward to sharing a sandwich and a beer with Muz, and teasing Muz's pretty wife, Mara, and their little girl.

Unlike his own one-room cabin, the village, a poor looking town made up of small houses set in haphazard rows along unpaved streets, enjoyed the unusual luxuries of running water and indoor plumbing. The streets had lights, and every home had electricity and a telephone.

Despite such modern conveniences, despite having a wife who had yellow hair and a pretty smile, Muz tended to eat too much and to brood too much during the short dark days of winter. Mara was a simpler, happier soul. Leander enjoyed her company, although she never read anything other than the labels on cans or the recipes in her cookbooks. Neither she nor her husband knew or cared who Leander really was or what he'd supposedly done. They just accepted him as one of them—someone who, like them, lived on an icy fringe of the world because he was running from demons he didn't much want to talk about. Nor did fame like his have a place in a simple village like theirs.

Lori, their little girl, was the same age as Christina, whom he tried never to think about although Dean Shaw, his agent in New York, sent her mother a large support check every month and a Christmas present every year.

In Muz's cabin Leander could throw off his solitude for an hour or two and get a glimpse of ordinary life.

In the beginning, Alaska had seemed a place of exile. But now as he sped through the snow-covered trees, the silent white land was like his writing—a refuge. He had lived alone so long, sometimes he felt he was only half-civilized. He had grown used to the quiet, to the peace, to the awesome power of nature.

With a dashing swirl of ice and snow, he skidded up to the largest cabin on either side by fish houses in which dried fish and sealskin bags of seal oil were stored along with nets, floats and other gear. Two other snowmobiles and their spare parts were nuzzled close to the front door.

Inside Muz's cabin a tiny Christmas tree stood beside racks of radio equipment that buzzed with static. Muz set the headset to his radio down onto his counter when Leander stomped inside and went to the fire where he tore off his snow-encrusted, mountain-squirrel parka and gloves.

Ivak padded over beside his master, and Leander ruffled the big dog's icy gray fur. When Leander turned away, Ivak whined and made a pitiful face. Then he rolled on his back, and put all four of his feet in the air, so Leander could check his paws for ice balls or injuries.

"Faker," Leander whispered as he knelt and lifted each frozen paw while Ivak panted and thumped his tail happily against the wooden floor.

"You should tie him out back with the other dogs," Muz growled. "You spoil that mutt."

When Leander began scratching that certain spot behind Ivak's right ear where the big dog's soul was lodged, the heavy tail thumped even more ecstatically.

"Yeah. I guess I do. But he's more than just a dog. And, hell, it's almost Christmas."

"Which reminds me. You got a big package from New York yesterday. And the usual from Juneau."

With a silent nod Leander indicated he'd heard. Withdrawing his hand from Ivak and studying the well-stocked gun rack to the left of the stove, he edged nearer to the fire.

His fingers felt numb. The cold had sapped even his abundant strength. It would take him a minute to recover. It always amazed him that Ivak could run the three miles across the ice and snow as if they were nothing. But then Sitka, his mother, had been a famous sled racer in her day. Such dogs could run sixty miles a day. They could trot at twelve miles an hour and lope at eighteen. Leander knew because he'd put that fact in a book once.

Mara placed two bulging brown packages and a mug of hot coffee on the table nearest Leander and a bowl of warm water on the floor for Ivak. Leander seized the mug, cupping it so that the heat of it seeped into his cold skin. The first package was from his secretary. The larger one was from his literary agent.

He unsheathed a hunting knife from his belt and slit open the package from New York first. Staples went flying and so did little popcorn bits of packing foam from the envelope. Ivak got up, pawing and sniffing every single popcorn with curious fascination. The page proofs of Leander's next novel fell out. So did three smaller envelopes.

He picked up the letters.

One was addressed in a childish hand to Mr. Santa Claus, c/o My Daddy, Mr. Leander Knight.

The second, which was also from Christina, was addressed solely to him.

For an instant his blood seemed to cease its flow.

Christina had never written him before.

Then his black gaze narrowed as he instantly recognized the neat, elegant loops of pretentious blue ink that sloped backward across the third velum envelope. *Heddy.*

Her handwriting seemed fake and pretentious. Heddy had learned to write like that after Tia had sent her to private school in Switzerland.

A muscle pulled in Leander's stomach as he remembered her messy childish scribble. She'd had some sort of fine-motor coordination problem and had failed handwriting in third grade, but he'd enjoyed getting notes from her back then even though they'd barely been legible.

Well, she damn sure wrote like a great lady now. Tia had won that battle, too.

He shoved his chair back so hard it nearly toppled, then strode over to the counter, leaned over it, grabbed Muz's bottle of brandy and poured a double shot into his coffee.

"Sure—help yourself, why don't you," Muz muttered grumpily without looking up.

"Thanks." Leander raised his mug in mock salute and shoved the bottle across the counter toward Muz, who caught it. "Run a tab, why don't you?"

Then returning to the table, Leander pushed Heddy's letter aside and took another long pull from his mug.

With his knife, he ripped open Christina's envelope. Inside were a Christmas card, a gilt-edged invitation to the Kinneys' annual Christmas party, a single, tissue-thin sheet of sloppily folded paper and a photograph of Christina and her mother.

His dark gaze glinted as he studied the snapshot. Heddy and Christina were wearing red-and-green pullover sweaters over crisply pressed jeans. They were standing in what looked like a wide river of golden grasses edged on both sides by ancient sand dunes on which grew dense oak and mesquite. They were blond, slim, and so alike somehow.

And so lovely with the sunlight and wind blowing in their hair. *And so beautifully dear to him, they put his soul in torment.*

Despite her jeans and youthfully trim figure, Heddy looked rich and sophisticated.

Why had he ever married her?

He ran his fingers through his black hair with a muttered curse. How many times had he told himself that he should have known from the first that Heddy Kinney had always been too rich for his blood. Still, even after he thrust their picture onto the table facedown, he couldn't shake off a powerful sense of despair and loss.

Eight years. How could it still hurt after eight years? It was a long time before he picked up his child's letter and began to read.

Big block letters ran crookedly up and down across the page, and since she'd used a pen and wasn't good at it, there were lots of scratch outs. Some of the *B*s and *P*s and *S*s were upside down and backward.

Dear Daddy, Hope you'll give Santa my letter since you live so close to the North Pole. Or, if you can't give it to him yourself, at least you oughta know his right address.

I sure hope you come to this party. I'm inviting you because my mommy said I could ask whoever I wanted and the only person I want in the whole world is you, Daddy.

I haven't written you before cause I wasn't good enough at writing. But I had to stay after school today cause I stole Attilla's chips at lunch, and my teacher helped me spell the hard words.

Guess what? I'm not an only child anymore. Which is good, because I got lonely with nobody to play with

and with you never here. Mommy dopted two kids.
They're fourth cousins. Or third. Twins. But they don't
look alike. Their mother and daddy were in a wreck. So
I guess I'm going to have a brother and a sister now.
Their names is Cleopatra and Attilla. Cleo cries a lot.
Mommy says cause she misses her mother. Attilla is
mean. He says he might run away. And I hope he does.

Please, please come to this party so that I can show
them that I do too have a daddy cause Attilla won't
believe it less you do.

                                    Luv, Christina Knight

P.S. I feel sorry for you cause you live in such a cold
place and you can't play outside.

He read the "Luv, Christina Knight" again and again. It
felt so natural, so good, her writing it with that childlike
trust as if she considered his love an unconditional thing.
Which he realized suddenly that it was. She seemed to feel
close to him even though she didn't know him.

She wanted to see him. To show him off. She was proud
of him.

It seemed incredible.

Equally incredible was his vague realization that he had
similar feelings. He *wanted* to see her. He was proud of her.

Remembering his own fatherless and motherless childhood, he could relate to her need *to prove* she had a daddy.

Leander reread the letter a dozen times, stunned and baffled that he was so touched. He thought he was alone, invulnerable. And then this child had reached out and touched
him. This child who seemed to take it for granted he would
know how to act around kids, that being a father was an
easy thing, that he'd fit right in because he was her daddy.

The party was a week before Christmas. He wondered how it would be if he just showed up.

Tia had already had one heart attack because of him.

But Heddy?

He flipped the photograph over and studied her blue eyes and corn silk hair. He pretty mouth still looked so kissable. Unbidden came the memory of how wild she had always been in bed.

Then he caught himself. She was Texas royalty. She thought he had used her as a step up the ladder to fame and fortune. He thought she had betrayed him by not believing in him. They had done one hell of a number on each other. For eight years he had told himself that he liked being alone, knowing that no one could get to him ever again the way she had.

No way could he go back. He didn't know the first thing about kids. And his relationship with Heddy was long over. All he'd ever known of normal family life was what little he'd had with Flora Janovich and Jim Bob.

He and Heddy had made their choices.

But now his kid was struggling to make hers.

Again he remembered how he'd longed for a father.

What the hell was he thinking about? He couldn't do Christina any good. Not when everybody thought he was even worse than any one of his fictional monsters. He had made the decision to stay out of her life a long long time ago—for her sake.

He finished his brandy-laced coffee before slitting open Heddy's letter.

Dear Leander,

I should have written you a long time ago and asked for a divorce, but until I found Marcus, it never seemed like the right time. And Christina liked the thought of

me still being married to you. Even if you weren't
here—

She misses having a father—

The rest of the letter blurred. But he got the gist.

There was a new man in her life. Marcus. He loved children. Her family, which meant Tia, loved Marcus. Heddy
wasn't really all that serious about Marcus yet, but there was
the possibility. It was time for all of them to move on with
their lives.

Leander wadded the letter and pitched it into the fire.
Even though she hadn't actually said it, Leander knew that
Marcus was some bloodless paragon who had been born
rich, who had lived a sane dull life and, therefore, had a
name that was unblemished by scandal and a soul un-
scarred by the ravages of poverty and illegitimacy and betrayal at the hands of his mother and then the woman he
loved.

Leander borrowed a pen and several sheets of paper from
Mara, but his large brown hand froze, and the tip of his pen
dug into the paper so hard after he wrote "Dear Christina"
that the sheet tore. He wadded it up and grabbed another.

Transfixed, he stared at the third blank page.

No words came. What could he say to this precious little
girl he didn't know but he felt so much for?

To the wife who wanted her freedom but whom he loved
still?

Loved? Did he love her?

And he had thought himself invulnerable and safe here.

He looked down at the picture. His wife and his daughter were holding each other, laughing. They looked so
happy—without him.

The lights on Muz's Christmas tree twinkled, mocking the
lonely darkness his childhood had carved inside him. Le-

ander had been born into the world alone and despised by his own mother. As a kid he'd wanted the same things all kids wanted—a family who loved him, friends and acceptance; and Christmas trees and Christmas presents. Not that he'd shown it. By the age of five he'd been so defiant and hostile that his foster home mothers had always given up on him and sent him back to the agency. When he was ten Flora Janovich had found him starving and hiding out along the creek that ran through her ranch. She'd run him down on horseback, lassoed him and thrown him kicking across her saddle, brought him back to her ranch house kitchen and fed him. Then she'd applied to the agency to become his foster mother. Early on she had proven she was even tougher than he was, refusing to take any of his nonsense. When he ran away, she always tracked him down. More than once they'd repeated that first ride with him bent double across her saddle. Finally he had realized that she really wanted him.

Flora and Jim Bob had given him so much, and, for a while, so had Heddy. But always Leander had known that he was different from other children—that he was more alone, that his own mother had abandoned him. No—that his own mother had thrown him away and left him to die. Then he'd lost Heddy.

He'd missed so much, so many years. So many Christmases. Everything. He had sworn to himself that never again would he reach out for the impossible.

A savage pulse throbbed behind his eyes as he imagined Heddy in another man's arms. As he imagined his child coming to think of another man as her father.

Damn brandy, he thought queasily, shocked at the depth of his emotion. All liquor ever did was open him up to the pain. So did writing, but in a different way.

Still, how could he hold on to a wife and child who were so far away? And there was no way he could go back. No way.

Not when he was despised as a murderer.

Not after the way Heddy had treated him.

She had thrown him away—as if he meant nothing—just as his mother had.

He forced his paralyzed fingers to move, to write a sentence that promised Heddy her freedom.

He kept it short.

Three words only, but they sucked him dryer than a nine-hundred-page novel.

"Divorce? Fine, Sugar." After that he could barely manage the rambunctious swirl of his gaudy signature.

He wrote Christina and said he couldn't come, but that she should give Attilla this letter so he would believe her.

He addressed both letters and gave them to Mara. When he returned to his table, he saw that Christina's letter to Santa Claus had fallen to the floor and lay between the radio equipment and the Christmas tree.

Indifferently Leander picked the envelope up and ripped it open.

The page began to shake as he read her first, childishly scrawled sentence.

He read no further.

But her plea to Santa changed everything.

Leander got up and stalked over to Muz and banged on the counter so Muz would look up. "If I go somewhere, will you take care of Ivak?"

At the mention of his name, Ivak shifted his golden eyes toward the two men and thumped his tail. Absorbed in his radio, Muz lifted his earphones only halfway off his head. "Juneau again? No problem."

"Farther than Juneau." *One helluva a lot farther.*

Leander paused, not wanting to say more. "You've gotta keep the ice out of his paws, and you can't let him stay out when it's too cold."

Muz's eyes rolled back, but his shaggy head lifted in an almost imperceptible nod. "It's damn silly the way you're so soft on that dog—"

"Yeah."

Good thing Muz didn't know what a fool he could be when it came to a woman.

Two

—

True, it was the week before Christmas, a hectic time for any successful shop owner. But that wasn't why the fitting rooms of Heddy's boutique were in an uproar.

True, Mary Ann, Heddy's sexy, redheaded assistant, who was writing a romance novel in her spare time, had had three very demanding customers trying on cocktail gowns for the past two hours. But other than the tapping of Mary Ann's spike heels as she rushed to and fro from the fitting rooms with chiffon gowns and rhinestone belts, other than the women's delighted whispers when they were thrilled, or their fretful sighs when they weren't, the four women scarcely made a sound.

No, the exuberant ruckus was due entirely to the children. Heddy and her seamstress, dear, plump Elvira Lopez, mother of eight, grandmother to twenty, had been closeted with Heddy's three darlings, doing fittings on the elf outfits that Tia had ordered from a catalogue. All three were to be dressed as Santa's elves in red suits with matching hats and shoes at the Kinney party.

The children had been wild even before they'd torn open the sacks that contained their suits and been metamorphosed into bright elves with tiny jingling bells.

In their new suits, everything—the other customers, the trinkets on the sale tables, Elvira—absolutely everything—became immensely more exciting. Tiring of making hand prints and nose prints and tongue prints on their reflections in the mirrors, they took off their hats and sank to the floor, peering under the cubicles, giggling as they watched the three ladies strip to their panty hose. After Heddy scolded them, they attacked one another.

"Make him stop, Mommy!" Christina said imperiously from the floor where she had been coloring when Attilla waggled a long red sleeve with jingling bells in front of her crayon. Not touching her. Not causing her to make a mistake. Just almost.

Attilla whose hair was as red as a carrot and as curly as corkscrews, had been full of himself all day. He had been whirling like a dervish in front of the mirror, dizzily slapping the other three children with his sleeves until Heddy had reprimanded him quite sharply. He was now prancing about like a boxer, his pants drooping and tangling around his ankles.

"Ouch!" Cleo screamed when she darted out of Attilla's way and stomped down onto a pin. "Aunt Heddy, get it out!" Big tears welled up in the child's huge, dark eyes.

"All right. All right," Heddy said, easing the pin out and holding it so that the weeping little girl with the ink black hair that fell like a curtain down her back could study it.

"If you would wear your shoes this wouldn't happen, Cleo."

Cleopatra was rubbing the tears off her cheeks. "I can't find them!"

"I think I saw you take them off under the Christmas tree."

Cleopatra was always taking her shoes off. Heddy was always looking for them.

"Kids, if all of you could just hold still, we'll be through in a jiffy," Elvira murmured.

How many times in the last hour had she said that? Heddy wondered.

Not that it mattered. The children paid not the slightest attention.

Attilla zoomed up to Cleo and swiped at her with his sleeve again. Not touching her hurt foot. Just teasing.

Maddened, Cleo shoved him into Christina whose purple crayon wriggled across Santa's plump pink face, ruining all her careful work. In a rage Christina yanked three orange corkscrews of hair. Attilla pinched both girls, and all three toppled like bowling pins.

"Attilla!" Heddy cried.

"Mrs. Knight, I think I can sew the outfits without fitting them."

"Bless you dear, talented Elvira."

Cleo was rubbing her foot and crying again, and the doorbell buzzed, which meant more customers. Christina, who had a flare for badly timed drama, chose that moment to look up from her coloring book and say softly, "Guess what! My daddy is coming to our Christmas party!"

Despite the confusion, the phrase *my daddy is coming* registered.

Heddy spun. "He's what?"

"Attilla didn't believe I really had a daddy so I wrote him and invited him. My teacher helped me."

"Christina—you had no right."

"You said I could ask whoever I wanted to."

"Whomever."

"Whomever," Christina repeated ungraciously.

"But I didn't mean *him*."

"If you don't let him come, I'll hate you forever and ever." Christina picked up her coloring book and stomped out of the room.

"Christina!"

They exchanged heated glances. Then Christina just ran faster.

They were outside now, mother and daughter, their matching golden heads huddled on the bench on the wide sidewalk in front of Heddy's shop. A single, very bright star, glowed in the purpling twilight sky.

Elvira was inside, helping the other elves get dressed. The sounds of their hilarity were muted by distance and glass windows, by the ringing of a bell by a fat woman across the street soliciting donations.

Christina was a sensational seven-year-old. She had very blue eyes, bluer even than Heddy's; translucent skin and a delicate bone structure that lent to her every movement a fluid, ballerina grace. She was an original—fey and dramatic or imperiously bossy—depending on her mood.

"I can't believe you wrote your daddy, honey."

"I wrote 'cause you wrote him about Marcus."

Heddy blushed, wondering how much Christina, who was a precocious reader, had understood. "Yes, I did write him."

Christina's eyes blazed rebelliously, yet she was very pale. "Are you going to marry Marcus?"

"I—I— We haven't talked about it," she said gently. "Right now Marcus and I are just friends."

"Good."

"Marcus loves children. He's very nice—"

Christina stiffened and thrust her chin higher, and Heddy was reminded of how she had rebelled when her family had tried to force her to be friends with children other than Leander.

Teasingly Heddy touched the defiant chin. "Honey, I just don't want you to be disappointed when your daddy doesn't come."

"He'll come," Christina stated with absolute faith.

Once, Heddy, too, had believed in Leander, even though her family had warned her against him. He had broken her heart.

"Honey, I—I don't think he can. He lives a very long way from here. He hasn't been back since— He and I, we made a deal—"

"He will. 'Cause I want him to so much. 'Cause I wrote Santa, too, and told him I wanted my daddy to come home for Christmas. Santa can make anything happen."

"Not this, honey."

"Then how come that guy from New York called and said—"

Heddy was about to argue, but a horn tooted, impatiently, and Christina looked past her and jumped up when she saw her great-grandmother's blue Lincoln. "Tia..."

As the automatic window on the passenger side lowered, Christina ran eagerly to the car, squealing when she saw the Christmas presents piled high on the back seat.

"Is one for me, Tia? Is—"

Tia's silver head nodded and she smiled. Her wrinkled face was alight at the sight of Christina.

"Which one, Tia? Which one? *Please* . . . Tell me."

Tia was as devoted a great-grandmother as she had been a grandmother. She supervised every detail of Christina's life.

Heddy felt a pang of guilt. The reason Tia was so overly concerned was because she believed she had failed with Heddy.

Deciding she'd have to talk to Christina later, Heddy got up reluctantly, spoke to Tia and then went inside to get the other children. She had forgotten Tia had promised to drive them to have ice cream at the Dairy Princess and then to the ranch after she finished shopping so Heddy could work late.

"I hope he does come," Mary Ann said dreamily from behind the cash register after Tia had driven away with the children.

Mary Ann had sold more merchandise today than she ever had before. Even though she had a talent for putting rich women into flattering outfits they would never have had the nerve to choose themselves, her mind was never really on the shop. When she wasn't flirting, she was daydreaming about her novel.

"You hope *who* comes?" Heddy asked, wishing Mary Ann would concentrate on closing out the day's receipts.

Mary Ann punched buttons haphazardly on the cash register, and long coils of tape began spilling from the machine and falling to the floor in messy tangles.

"You could be fanfolding the—" Heddy began.

"Your husband. I hope he—"

"He's not really my—"

"But he's a writer! And not just any writer!" Unconsciously Mary Ann stepped on the tape. "He's famous."

Heddy bit her lip. "Are you watching that tape?"

"Oh, sorry." Mary Ann moved aside. "I couldn't put *Midnight Eyes* down. I mean he's really talented at creating a brooding mood of horror."

"Yes..." Heddy's faint voice trailed into nothingness.

"You know I'm almost finished with my own book. Maybe he can tell me what I have to do to get it published.

I've heard you have to have an agent. You have to know people in New York. I bet he has connections—"

The cash register had quit clicking, and the thick white coils hung motionless. Not that Mary Ann noticed.

"He's not coming," Heddy said stonily as she punched a button to clear the machine.

"But Christina said she—"

Heddy ripped the tape out of the machine so savagely that it tore. Then she marched toward her desk and turned her slim back to Mary Ann. "He wouldn't dare."

But he did . . . dare.

Leander parked Jim Bob's truck a mile from the house, off the narrow ranch road and behind a tall hedge of salt cedar. Then he loped up the blacktopped drive. Keeping to the shadows of the stunted trees, he sneaked around to the back of the tall three-story mansion. There he waited for several guests to descend before he crept up the stairs to the darkened verandah and stared through the tall windows into the brilliantly lit ballroom.

Even though it was late December, and a norther was in the forecast, the air was damp and unpleasantly warm. A sharpening southeasterly breeze was gusting across the flat savannahs from the Gulf, snapping the party tents in the garden and rustling the palm fronds briskly.

It was so different from Alaska. And yet so familiar. So poignantly home, even after all the years.

He never dressed up in Alaska. His rented tuxedo bound him too snugly across his wide shoulders; his pleated shirt made his neck itch. He wanted nothing more than to rip at the starched collar and send studs flying.

A huge Christmas tree with sparkling white lights and silver bows stood in the center of the ballroom. Four huge chandeliers lit the room. Long tables that stretched against the far wall were laden with fancy pink linen and silver candelabra. Crystal bowls and plates were piled high with catered delicacies.

The three-piece band was loud, but Leander felt as cut off from the dancers as if he were encased in a glass bottle with no holes punched in the lid. Other than the beating of his heart, there was absolute silence. And no air.

The glittering people in the ballroom seemed to move noiselessly, without echoes. In their glittery world that was so far removed from his, they laughed easily, noiselessly. They belonged; they were happy while he was an outcast.

Then Heddy came into the room. Heddy with her radiant, glorious face, with her pale shimmering hair forming a halo around her face. She wore a red silk sheath that fit her like a glove. But no jewels. She was so stunning, her image burned into his retina with such absolute clarity that when he shut his eyes at her unbearable beauty, he saw her still.

His Heddy, his very own Heddy, lovely, warm and so much more alive than anyone else in that room. And yet beneath her beauty he sensed a sadness in her, a loneliness that mirrored his own.

The years they had been apart were as nothing to him. More than anything he wanted to go to her. He had to know whether her face would light up with joy or go dark with sorrow. Would she ache for his kisses or despise him? And he hated himself for the fierce burning need to know.

Leander took an involuntary step toward the door, intending to join her. Suddenly a tall blond man came out of nowhere and gathered her into his arms, sweeping her onto the dance floor and vanishing with her behind the Christmas tree.

It was then that Leander remembered that there was no way he could approach her without crossing a barrier of immense pain. She believed he was a murderer, and he almost loathed her for thinking him so low. He had built walls to protect himself, and he did not want to let them down.

The couple whirled around from the other side of the tree. That look of sadness had left her face. Flushed and laughing now, Heddy tilted her head up to her partner's whose lean golden features were warm and caressingly tender.

Leander drew a harsh breath and forced himself to study his adversary. The man appeared rich and dashing, his custom-made tux the height of style and tailoring. He danced flawlessly, with the confident air of a man who'd inherited his money. He had the affable appearance of someone who found life an easy voyage. He could offer the woman he chose what he himself possessed in abundance—happiness and security, acceptance by society. There were probably few women who could resist his charms when he chose to exert them. And Heddy, who placed her head against Marcus's elegant shoulder, did not look like she wanted to resist them.

The other guests stopped dancing and made a huge circle for the glamorous couple who spun faster and faster around the large tree under the sparkling chandeliers. When the onlookers began to clap enthusiastically to the beat of the music, Leander's heart began to hammer at the same desperate tempo.

Because of this man, Heddy wanted to divorce him.

He left the dark verandah and went to the front of the house and joined the party.

When Leander strode tigerlike into the ballroom, a dozen pair of eyes turned and watched him.

Dramatically tall and broad-shouldered with his piercing dark gaze, he was used to stares, especially from women, the most beautiful of women—at his publishers' parties—everywhere. But this was different.

There were horrified gasps from the women and hostile scowls from the men.

"Murderer," someone hissed.

The cruel word tore through Leander.

"That bastard's one scary guy."

Leander forced a tight smile when he saw Tom Yates.

"Of all the nerve. Do you think Heddy knows he's here?"

More heads turned his way.

Leander felt like he was a kid in school again—friendless and helpless, about to be set up by Tom. As sheriff, Tom had made Leander's life a living hell before he'd left town. Leander knew he'd better make his move—fast.

"Oh my," the beautiful redhead in a low-cut green gown who was clinging to Tom cooed. "Will you get a load of that? Rich and famous and dangerously drop-dead gorgeous to boot."

"The key word for that lowlife is—*dangerous*. I'd like to give him the boot. Watch yourself, M.A., or you may be the one to drop dead next," Yates warned.

"Oh, pooh, Tom! The way you hate him, if you'd had a shred of evidence, you'd have put him away for life!"

"He hid behind Tia—"

"I thought a man was innocent till proven—"

"In the eyes of the so-called law maybe."

"Well, I told Heddy I simply had to speak to him if he came!"

Leander hesitated at the sound of Heddy's name. Which gave the redhead with the amazing cleavage time to pounce on him.

"Mr. Knight! I've read all your books! I absolutely adored *Midnight Eyes!* I can't believe you really came! Welcome home."

When she seized his hand, Leander tensed. She was sexier than hell. Not that he felt particularly interested. He was too aware of the buzzing whispers around them, and far too aware of Heddy.

"I'm sorry," he said, trying to shrug loose. "Do I know you?"

"You could..." She thrust her amazing chest even closer. "I'm Mary Ann!" she gushed.

Leander shook his head, puzzled. "Sorry?"

"I work for Heddy—in her shop. But, you see, I'm not just a salesgirl. I'm a writer, too. Romances. Or at least I want to be. I'm just starting. I thought maybe you could tell me how I could sell—"

An unpublished writer, and a romance writer at that—a desperate breed. He'd met her type hundreds of times in the past—at signings, in bookstores, at parties. She was one of those predictable creatures who could become instantly infatuated with any writer whom she believed possessed the secret of publication. As if publication were some sort of magic attainment.

Imperceptibly he relaxed. Both her gushing admiration and her questions were routine. Hell, it wasn't that he didn't empathize. He could be as neurotic and insecure about his writing as anybody. He felt vaguely guilty that his only real interest in her was her connection to Heddy.

She began describing every detail of her manuscript. He nodded mechanically, hoping he'd plastered a suitably sympathetic expression on his face as he strained for more glimpses of Heddy.

The glamorous couple whirled from behind the Christmas tree.

Did Heddy have to stroke that rich wimp's throat in front of the whole world? Did she really have to wind a strand of his yellow hair around her fingertip? Had she forgotten that she was still married—to him?

The voluptuous redhead asked who his agent was, where he got his spooky ideas—the usual. Leander answered her.

She said if someone would only read her book, would only tell her what was wrong with it—

Hardly aware that he spoke, his entire attention focused on Marcus's hand wandering through Heddy's golden hair, on Heddy nuzzling her head against Marcus's shoulder, Leander promised to read the book.

When the couple vanished again, and Mary Ann squeezed Leander's hand in thanks and pressed her incredible bosoms closer, he wondered what exactly he'd promised her.

The beautiful couple swirled out from behind the Christmas tree once again. The crowd parted. Suddenly as Mary Ann was kissing his cheek—Heddy seemed, at last, to feel the burning pull of Leander's gaze.

Slowly, as if in a dream, she turned.

Her eyes locked with his.

It was as if they were the only two people in the room. The music faded to a murmur.

His heart began to beat erratically, and not because the writer had draped her sexy body all over him.

It was because of Heddy that he couldn't breathe.

Apparently Heddy couldn't get her breath, either.

Numbly he watched her hand go to her mouth in horror.

Numbly he watched her try to push herself free of Marcus. If Leander didn't stop her and fast, she was going to run before he had a chance to talk to her.

Mary Ann was happily babbling as Leander said an impatient goodbye. Then he rushed toward Heddy, reaching her just as she was about to run.

The music stopped in the middle of a measure, punctuating the dramatic moment.

Tom Yates and his hostile gossips buzzed as angrily as a swarm of killer bees.

On the other side of the ballroom, a pale Tia placed a shaky hand over her heart.

Thunderstruck, Heddy stood as if paralyzed while Leander slowly took her slim hand and forced her into his arms, dragging her against his hard body.

Close up, Heddy looked even better to Leander than she had from the verandah. Her warm flesh was creamy soft and seemed to flow over her bones. Her trembling lips were full; she smelled like fresh flowers after a rain. Her long sleek legs, which were aligned against his, seemed to go on forever.

He felt the heat of her as he drew her closer. The excitement of her. And he got hot in spite of himself.

As he drank in that first long look before her eyes frosted over, he knew that she was every bit as lonely as he, and that no matter how she might pretend otherwise, she had missed him as terribly as he'd missed her.

Then Heddy's eyes went bluer than polar ice chips.

Several of Tia's friends including a man dressed as Santa Claus were leading Tia to Santa's throne where she collapsed.

Marcus was the first to recover. "What is the meaning of this?" he demanded. "I say—"

"Do you mind if I dance with my wife," Leander drawled in a softly resonant, well-modulated tone that was somehow dangerous.

"Your what?" Marcus stared at Heddy, who had gone white and was clinging to Leander as if she might faint.

"But we...we're getting a divorce," Heddy said furiously.

"We're still married, damn it," Leander repeated.

Marcus bowed his head politely and backed out of their way as Leander dragged her nearer and signaled curtly to the musicians to begin.

"What if I don't want to dance with you," Heddy whispered, yanking at his hands.

"Don't make a scene. Wherever you go, I'll follow." He swept her with the music into a quick turn.

"Why?" she asked. "Why are you doing this?"

"You wrote. So did Christina."

"I wrote for a divorce."

"She invited me to come tonight."

"But... she's just a child."

"Exactly. Our child. It's Christmas—a special time for us. Maybe I felt homesick."

"How could you, when you know what people think of you—"

"Yes," he said, unable to conceal his dark pain as he glared down at her. "And I know who made them think it."

"Leander—"

They were dancing now. The long windows that were decorated with ivy and mistletoe and red ribbons were swirling past them. So were three bright elves who were madly jumping up and down in excitement in Santa's chair. One elf had long golden braids and blue eyes.

And then suddenly Leander saw Tia slumping weakly into the big red chair, looking paler and more fragile than Leander had ever seen her.

The old lady watched them with dark, hooded eyes, like a tragic queen at the center of a kaleidoscope. Her arched brows lifted faintly. She was struggling to hold her chin high, to smile calmly, to maintain some semblance of regal control, but she was trembling.

The elves were dancing. Other couples began to dance.

Leander couldn't see Tia any longer, but he could not forget her any more than he could forget the hostile crowd massing around them. Tia controlled the town. Even though she had pretended to back him all those years ago, she had deliberately made everyone hate him.

Maybe she was older and frailer, but nothing had changed. All the old forces that had driven him away and destroyed his reputation and marriage still existed. He looked down at Heddy's pale face and saw that she was still afraid of him. And it was her fear—not the town's hatred or Tom Yates and his goons constantly harassing him—that had driven him away.

"You shouldn't have come," Heddy said, but breathlessly now. "They hate you. They might even hurt you."

"So what," he said in a deep dark voice. "At least then you'd be rid of me."

"I don't want that."

Her glance lifted to his, and in her eyes he saw some strange emotion. When he gently folded her closer, she didn't stop him.

They danced as they had always danced, as if they were made to dance only with each other, and their dancing brought that old familiar intimacy, that natural easiness that had always been between them even though they were in public.

"I didn't want to feel anything for you," she said several minutes later, her eyes still shining strangely, her fear of him gone now.

"I know." But he felt caught in the same spell. He didn't care what the whole world thought of him, if only she—

She had turned her back on him. No way was he going to make a fool of himself over her again.

But the passionate music carried him on magic wings, suspending reality.

"I don't ever want to stop dancing," she said, her feet floating through the steps.

He whirled her out onto the moonlit terrace where they danced in the warm night air and deserted shadows. One star was brighter than all the others. Lightning crackled to the north. The music was muted now, but the magic closeness between Heddy and himself held.

At last he stopped and was not surprised when her arms tightened around him. An odd shiver darted through him when he saw that she was crying.

"I've had dreams like this sometimes, of you coming back, of everything being like it was when we were so happy," she said through her tears. "It's so good to see you, Leander."

"It's good to see you too," he said gently before he thought. "You're still the most beautiful—" He broke off.

"I thought we'd be like strangers."

"I hoped we would be."

She touched his raven hair with the tips of her fingers—as she had touched Marcus's. But Leander forced himself not to think of that.

"You're beautiful, too," she said. "But...but we hurt each other."

"Yes. Don't think about it," he commanded roughly. For some reason he was no longer in the mood to dwell on bitter memories.

"All right," she murmured, melting into him on a sigh, her closed lashes feathery crescents against her pale cheeks, her scent heavy and fragrant.

Neither of them knew how or when their lips came together and fused in that warm frantic darkness. Above them high clouds were whirling. Lightning flashed against the northern horizon.

Neither of them heard or cared when the music stopped. She was kissing him with an ardor he couldn't resist. His heart was beating like a drum. When his mouth fastened on hers with a greedy passion as if he wanted to devour her, she opened her lips to his endlessly.

He knew he should stop, but he had neither the will nor the self-control to resist her.

It was she who finally pulled away, quivering, smiling up at him in that beguiling way that compelled every emotion in his soul. His body tensed when she moved closer and her moist lips found the base of his throat and began to nibble. His heart slammed in fast, heavy strokes.

"It's been awful...without you," she muttered, shuddering against his collar, her hands clutching him now as if she would never let him go, her warm breath on his skin firing shafts of desire through him. "Awful. God, how I missed you, Leander."

"I don't want a divorce—not yet, anyway," he said a long time later, admitting too much because he was drugged from the taste of her honeyed lips and his own hot need.

"It's not that easy." But her mouth was seeking his frantically. In the next breath the wet wildness of her tongue inside his lips again brought ecstasy. He closed his eyes and surrendered to the bittersweet pleasure of her.

When coyotes yelped in the faraway gloom, nostalgia washed through him. He was a kid again, and she had sneaked out to meet him in the oak mott near the house. She loved him. There had been no pain then. Only the wild glorious beauty of her. Only the naive, youthful certainty he'd felt every time she'd sworn she was his destiny.

He held her tightly, his loins aching now for far more than chaste kisses, his soul aching for an end to his loneliness.

She wrapped her arms around him, as caught as he was in their dangerous embrace until Tia's thin voice shattered their dream.

"Heddy!"

Guiltily Heddy pushed Leander away, her face blanching in the moonlight.

"What do you think you're doing?"

Heddy's low whisper was shaky. "Oh, God..."

Leander grew cold. As always, one word from Tia could destroy everything Heddy might feel for him.

"Oh, God, Tia. I—I don't know," Heddy said.

Tia was leaning heavily on Tom Yates's arm as she walked toward Leander, her eyes icy, her imperious nose high.

She still thought she was a queen and he was dirt.

Leander swore viciously under his breath.

Reality was back with a vengeance.

Again Leander noticed that Tia couldn't walk without support. It seemed an effort for her just to keep that haughty lift to her chin so she could stare down her nose at him. Her bones were more prominent; her pale skin was a web of wrinkles. The thin hand she pressed to her heart was shaking.

But before Leander could ask the older woman if she was all right, a mischievous elf with bouncing blond braids skipped up. She was trailed by two other elves.

"See, Attilla," the lead elf taunted the freckled-faced hellion behind her. "I told you so!" And in a softer voice of pure awe and intense love—to Leander alone—Christina said, "Merry Christmas, Daddy!" Softer still and warmer, "I saw you kissing Mommy! Does that mean you're going to stay? Oh, I hope so. 'Cause that's what I want."

Leander sank to his knees. He felt weak and tired suddenly. Yet his heart thundered at the sight of the golden little girl who approached him with such imperious confidence. He was thrilled when Christina crawled into his arms, usurping her mother's spot. Without a shred of shyness, she snuggled close and pressed her childish mouth against his ear so that only he could hear her secret wish, "I want you to stay with me and Mommy more than anything in the whole world."

Her warm breath tickled his earlobe. Her slim fingers tightened possessively around his neck as if she assumed he was hers to command.

His throat was too choked for him to answer.

"Christina, it's past your bedtime," Tia said frigidly. "Heddy, dear, I'm afraid Marcus is looking quite lost without you. I really think you should—"

"Of course. I'll go at once, Tia."

Heddy had barely managed a robotic half turn before Leander's husky voice stopped her.

"No," he said quietly. "Stay." He rose easily even though he was still holding Christina and extended a hand to his wife.

"Please, don't go, Mommy," Christina begged. "Not if Daddy doesn't want you to."

Three

————

The freshening wind had changed direction. High silver clouds, backlighted by the moon, were rolling to the north where occasional bursts of lightning exploded.

Not that Leander, whose eyes were glued on his wife's white face, was thinking about the weather.

"Heddy— Don't go." His voice was no more than a whisper, but its gentle warmth stopped her cold.

"Are you forgetting how this smooth-talking, scary bastard married you for your money and then killed your daddy, girl?" Tom snarled. "How he got rich and famous writing that book that made the Kinney name the biggest joke in Texas?"

Heddy paled.

Rage blazed through Leander that she could believe that. "Damn it, Yates!"

"No, Daddy!" Christina whispered frantically when she felt Leander tense. "He's the *sheriff*. He's got a *big* gun."

Leander said tightly, "That's a damned lie, Yates, and someday when you've completely ruined things between Heddy and me and Christina, I'll probably be able to prove it."

"Yeah. Right. Maybe Heddy and your kid'll buy that, but it'll take more than a few hot words to make me see you as a saint."

"This is a family matter, Tom," Tia warned in her soft commanding voice. "We'll settle it ourselves like we always do."

"By condemning me to a lonely hell in Alaska without Heddy or Christina for the rest of my life. I know your tactics, Tia. You won't say a word against me. You won't have to. But you'll have Heddy feeling guilty and believing the worst of me again. From the first day you ever saw me you set about trying to make her see me as her inferior."

"Which you are," Tia said faintly.

Heddy was staring from Leander to Tia in confusion.

Damn those blind eyes of hers for not seeing the truth. Those gorgeous luminous windows into her softhearted soul. Leander hated the way he could see both Heddy's longing for him as well as her fear of him. He hated the way the two things twisted inside him like a knife and her pain became his.

"I don't know who to believe," Heddy said at last.

Leander mood darkened. "So what's new?"

As always Tia took charge. "If you're confused, Heddy, dear, imagine how Christina must feel," Tia said gently. "Take her inside. Leander, you'd better leave. Christina—"

"When you were a kid, you never let anybody tell you what to think," Leander said wearily to Heddy.

"I only acted like that at school to impress you," Heddy sighed. "Leander, maybe Tia is right, at least for tonight. It's late. We can talk tomorrow."

Tomorrow. But would she listen? Tia was so clever—so smooth. She always convinced people that she was acting in the best interests of everybody, especially Christina. In the past, he'd been too confrontational. Tia had used his hot-headed outbursts against him. Maybe it was smarter to appear to back off tonight. If he did, he might have a better chance with Heddy.

Leander nodded and then sank to his knees, saying bleakly to Christina, "You'd better do as Tia says—for now. Go on inside with your mother."

"But, Daddy, I don't want to!" Christina declared passionately.

"Neither do I, but I'll be back to see you both tomorrow, honey."

"Promise?"

He looked up at Heddy as he spoke to Christina. "Honey, the only reason I came to Texas was 'cause you asked me to. I'm not going to just leave—"

"I want you to meet Mayflower, my dog. She's part coyote."

"And I want to meet her. I like dogs."

"She used to be my only friend—before Attilla and Cleo came. She kills rattlesnakes. Even great big ones—"

"Tomorrow, honey—"

"She bites their necks and shakes 'em—"

Leander grew quiet, and he took his time straightening Christina's elf hat, tweaking it so he rang the little bells and made her smile. He traced the soft length of a golden braid with his thumb. Then very gently he pushed her away and rose.

But Christina stared up at him, her eyebrows drawing together to form one ferocious brow, her bottom lip sticking out like a bulldog's.

"Go with your mother, sweetheart," he ordered, his voice soft.

She sucked in a huge defiant breath.

"Christina—" Heddy begged.

Grudgingly Christina began backing slowly until she came within inches of her mother whose hand she then crossly refused. But when Heddy tried to coax her toward the house, the child didn't budge.

Only when Heddy turned back toward Leander did Christina bound after her.

Heddy put a soft anxious hand on his forearm. "Leander—"

He couldn't have been more stunned when she said, "You'll be careful? There are people around here who don't like you much."

Those gorgeous blue eyes of hers again, working their magic on him as she stared up at him. Christina was looking at him, too, with identical blue eyes.

Heddy was worried. For his sake. As she'd been that first day at school. As she'd been throughout their childhoods.

For eight long years who had ever given a damn whether he lived or died. No human being.

Only Ivak, his husky.

And his publisher and agent, whom he rarely saw. They cared, but for financial reasons.

Nothing on earth but Heddy's soul-deep gaze and his daughter's pinched face could have shown him what a lonely, pathetic existence his life in Alaska without them had been.

Before he thought, his large brown hand gently cupped her chin. She was such a little thing. Ever since she'd rebelled and married him, she'd had a self-destructive tendency to try to make up to Tia by letting her bully her. Heddy was trying to raise three children without a man to help her. He knew she had a tendency to work too hard when she wasn't happy.

Tenderly he brushed a golden tendril out of her eyes. "I'll be careful, Sugar," he promised. "Now you go on. I'll call you tomorrow."

She smiled, a sad smile that stung him the same way her eyes had.

"You too, Christina," he whispered.

When Marcus met them at the door, Leander whirled on Tia. Forgetting the old woman's frailty, he said bitterly, "You've been running the show a long, long time, Tia. Did you ever stop and ask yourself if you know what the hell you're doing?"

Marcus was folding Heddy into his arms in the doorway.

Tia's color had heightened. "I know exactly what I'm doing. You'd better go, Pepper. You shouldn't have come. And don't you come back. I won't have you snooping around on this ranch, pestering Heddy, confusing her. You've made her miserable. She's better off with Marcus."

"Last I heard, Tia, I was still her husband."

"Stay away from her."

Stonily furious—hell, worse than that—green with jealousy at the thought of Heddy obediently returning to Marcus, Leander turned his back on Tia and stomped down the steps that led from the terrace to the drive. But he didn't head for Jim Bob's truck as she'd ordered him to. As soon as he was out of her sight, he doubled back and took the trail through the high brown grasses into the brush that led to the ravine where he'd found Barret's decaying body all those years ago.

For eight long years Leander had wanted to forget the nightmare that had destroyed his life.

No longer.

Tonight he wanted to remember—everything.

When he reached the steep-sided cliff that plunged to a dry creek bed, the past came back with a vengeance.

The first sign of trouble had been the gunshots. The instant he'd heard them, Leander had spurred his palomino, galloping away from the cows he'd been working, reining in only after he'd gotten close enough to catch the boys' high-pitched, quavery voices.

"You...you reckon somethin's dead down there?" Mickey McKamey had asked.

"Stinks mighty bad. Why don't you find a stick or something and crawl down there and poke it."

"No—might be more snakes. Maybe a whole swarming nest of them this time. You do it!"

"Chicken!"

"I ain't no chicken, Amos!"

"What's going on here, boys?" Leander had shouted as he'd ridden up. "You boys been shooting?"

Both boys, who had been leaning down and peering avidly into the ravine, jumped and tried to tuck their guns under their belts. Not that it was any use their trying to hide them. Leander, a dead shot himself, had eyes like a hawk.

"You boys been poachin' on the ranch again?" Leander demanded sternly. "How many times do I have to—"

"We didn't hit nuthin', Mr. Knight. Not anything you'd mind about leastways."

"That wasn't exactly what I asked, now, was it, Amos?"

"Show 'im that rattle you got in your back pocket, Amos," Mickey ordered.

After Amos dug out the rattle, Leander leaned across his saddle scabbard and took it.

"It's got nineteen joints! That sucker was as big around as your arm!"

"Where'd you shoot him?"

"Over there by your windmill. He was lying on a big rock."

Leander turned the rattle over in his palm, studying it like a virtuoso examining a fine instrument. "Very impressive." He looked Amos in the eye. "How far?"

Amos beamed. "Thirty feet. One round."

Leander nodded approvingly and returned the rattle. "So—you two been shooting up the windmill blades again?"

Both boys flushed.

"How many times do I have to tell you boys not to come on Kinney Ranch with those guns?"

"There's something mighty dead down there, Mr. Knight," Mickey said to distract him again. "Something mighty big. Maybe a cow— Stinks something awful. I was about to crawl down and check it out when you come up."

And as Leander's palomino shifted closer to the edge of the rocky ledge, the wind changed and Leander caught a whiff of a powerful stench that almost gagged him. The brush must have been too thick for the buzzards to get to whatever was down there and pick it clean.

Dismounting and scrambling down through the dirt and rocks and prickly pear cactus, heedless of the rough branches tearing at his shirt and chaps, Leander had already known it wasn't going to be a cow.

He'd known—even before he saw his Beretta half-buried in the gravel and sandy loam.

Even before he saw the skeletal hand that had been gnawed half off by coyotes thrusting up from the rocks.

Even before he recognized Barret's navy checked shirt—the

one he'd been wearing the afternoon they'd quarreled in the library.

"Boys, y'all get on back to the big house and call the sheriff," he'd said in a harsh low tone. "Hurry up now. You bring Mr. Yates back here—right away. Along with the coroner and an ambulance."

"Gosh almighty, Mr. Knight! What's down there?"

"You and Mickey just get, Amos, and do like I said."

Leander hadn't touched the Beretta; he'd just knelt and stared at it. Picking up a handful of sand and sifting it through his fingers, he'd known for sure the gun was his. Just like he knew even before Heddy came flying and stumbling down into the ravine like a wild woman with Tia right behind her that everybody would think for sure, now, that he'd gone and killed Barret in a rage. Because it was a well-known fact that Barret had hated Leander with an insane passion ever since he'd married Heddy. Just like it was a well-known fact that Barret had berated him constantly and that Leander had a dangerous temper and was better than anybody with a pistol....

All these years after the fact, staring into the dark nothingness, it was easy for Leander to see where he'd gone wrong.

God. He stared up at the big black sky. The clouds parted. The constellation Orion was straight over his head.

If only he'd gotten up and walked out on the old man that awful afternoon in the library. If only they hadn't quarreled.

Leander had been paying the ranch bills, when Barret had stormed in and started accusing him of getting a bang out of signing all those big checks.

"That's not your money, boy. And this isn't your ranch. And it never will be. Not if I have anything to do with it."

Leander's tight-lipped silence had made Barret angrier.

"You think you're high-and-mighty now—sitting there under my granddaddy's portrait? At his desk? I've seen the way you lord it over all the vaqueros. Well, you're nothing but a low-born bastard. Nothing but a two-bit, trashy gold-digging hustler who married up. You aren't half good enough to be married to a Kinney. You're stupid and lazy—the way you sit around staring out the window and writing all the time. You don't know the first thing about ranching or anything else that counts. Everybody laughs at me 'cause of you, boy."

"Why the hell did you come back early from San Antonio?" Leander had demanded, too furious to look up.

"You quit college. The only way you could think to make it was to marry my damn fool daughter."

"I quit school to help Mrs. Janovich," Leander rasped. "I've been going to night school ever since. I'll get a degree—no thanks to you. And from the looks of these bills, I know a helluva lot more about ranching than you do. And for what it's worth, I love your daughter."

"Her and who else? Damn it, Knight, you and I both know the way women chase you. You cheat on Heddy every chance you get. It's in your sorry blood."

"You shut your mouth, old man."

"Why? You just married her because of the ranch. Why don't we finish this once and for all? I'll give you what you really want. And you can go."

Leander should have walked out. Instead he had shoved the account books aside so recklessly they'd crashed to the floor along with the lamp. "All right, let's finish it."

Barret grabbed the open checkbook and then threw it down and went to the wall safe. "No, I'll pay you in cash—however much you want—if you'll just clear out and never come back."

"Damn it, Barret. There's not enough money in that safe to buy me."

"Then I'll go to the bank and get more."

"Get this, old man—I married her, and I intend to stay married to her!"

"No, you get this!" Barret had swung his fist into Leander's jaw so fast that Leander had crashed to the floor. Then Barret had jumped him.

Even then Leander hadn't fought back. He'd only defended himself, crossing his arms in front of his face to ward off the worst blows, crashing into the desk when the older man threw him against it again. Then he fell into the broken glass from the lamp on the floor, into the bookcases. Though Leander was younger, Barret had attacked him like a demon, his maniacal fists pounding into him. Finally Barret had picked up the broken lamp and swung it straight at Leander's face.

In that last second before he ducked, Leander had been sure Barret had gone completely crazy and was going to kill him. Then the lamp smashed into the back of his head, and he had blacked out. But when Barret had raised the lamp again Heddy had come in and screamed.

Everything might have been okay if the servants had kept their mouths shut. But, no, they had told how Barret had staggered out of the library covered in Leander's blood, about how Leander had suffered a concussion and gotten the worst of it, about how the desk had been turned over and the lamp broken.

About how Leander had called the old man crazy, and Barret had screamed that theirs was a fight to the death right before he hit him with the lamp. And every time the story was retold, it got worse.

When Barret didn't come home that night, people got curious. When Leander's gun turned up missing, they started talking.

Worst of all, to Leander, had been that Heddy was so shaken by the fight. She'd been guiltily withdrawn as she'd tended Leander's injuries. Then Tia had come into their bedroom and told them that Leander's gun and Barret were both gone and asked Leander if he had any idea where they were.

He'd retorted caustically, "How would I know, Tia? He hit me so hard I've been in bed all afternoon."

"Oh, so... that's your story," Tia had said, staring pointedly past him to Heddy.

The servants had reported everything. When Barret didn't return, tension built both on the ranch and in town.

Leander stared into the dark ravine and forced himself to remember the awful sense of doom that had engulfed him after Amos and Mickey had hightailed it back to the house while he'd waited with the body.

He'd stared at his gun and sifted sand endlessly through his fingers until he'd heard Heddy's terrified scream above him. She'd stumbled and fallen down the cliff, practically landing in his arms.

With a single frightened gasp she'd pushed him away and crawled through the dirt to her father's body.

Staring into his open lifeless eyes, she had begun to sob. "Oh, Daddy, you look so dead."

Tia had simply asked, "What's your Beretta doing here, Leander?"

Heddy had stared at the gun and then at him, her eyes dazed, unfocused. "Tia's right. If I hadn't married you, this never would have happened." Her low tone was more guilt stricken than ever.

"I didn't kill him, Heddy."

"I—I wish I could believe you. I'd give anything, if only I could, but Tia—"

"Damn Tia, what does she—"

"Heddy," Tia said, "I want you to believe him. Leander is your husband, and if we don't stand behind him and convince our friends and family to do the same, who else will?"

"I—I... But you—"

"Do you want Leander to go to prison?"

Heddy buried her head in her hands.

"He will, if we aren't strong," Tia said. "People will say he married you for the ranch and killed your father for the same reason. Do you think your father would have wanted more scandal?"

Heddy's face was white when she looked from Tia to him and then back to Tia.

"Damn it," Leander said. "I didn't shoot him. Neither of you have to cover up a damn thing."

When he reached for Heddy, she backed toward Tia.

"This is going to be difficult for all of us, Leander," Tia said, her voice very soft, almost exultant as she petted Heddy's bowed head. "But we are both behind you completely."

"The hell you are."

Then the sheriff had come and made a pretense of investigating the shooting. Friends and relatives had gathered in the big house and helped Tia plan an extravagant funeral that even included the governor.

The guests, some of whom stayed for more than a week, were supportive of Tia and Heddy, and of Leander, at least on the surface, but their incessant small talk and guarded silences when he was around wore on Leander's badly frayed nerves.

Heddy was thin and pale—guilt stricken because of her belief that her marriage to Leander was the cause of her father's death.

He overheard a guest say sympathetically to Tia, "It's so wonderful what you're doing for him and Heddy. I don't know if I could stand by someone who—"

"It's not easy—you see—tying myself to him forever. If only Heddy had stayed married to Bro."

Then the guests were gone. Barret was buried beside his father, and the big house was empty and lonely and more tension filled than ever. Heddy was unable to let go of her feelings of guilt and love him again.

Unless forced, Heddy would have nothing to do with Leander. If he walked into a room, she ran from it. She spoke to him only when he asked her a direct question. She would listen to his explanations and say nothing.

Yates came every day. He made it clear he detested Leander, just as he made it clear he would handle everything the way Tia wanted. Thus, Yates's investigation was at best halfhearted. Still, to pacify the gossips who were yammering for Leander's hide, Yates put a deputy on Leander's tail every time Leander left the ranch.

At first Leander hoped that Yates might accidentally stumble onto some shred of evidence that might exonerate him. But Yates allowed his deputies to contaminate the crime scene. Then they lost the bullet that had killed Barret as well as the coroner's report. When Tia replaced the servants who had gossiped, and Yates didn't even try to find them, everybody knew the Kinneys had bought the "justice" they wanted.

"Pepper did it, or Tia wouldn't be working so hard to protect him," they all agreed.

When somebody shot at Leander one night, Yates had stuck his finger through the bullet hole in Leander's truck

and laughed. "Damn shame whoever did this wasn't as talented with a pistol as you, Knight!"

Even after Heddy moved out of their bedroom, Leander
had hung on a while longer, hoping for a miracle. Finally
they quarreled for the last time, and he had walked.

He had returned to Kinney once and begged her to come
with him and start over somewhere else. But she wouldn't
leave Tia. Months later when Heddy had come to New York
seeking a reconciliation, Leander had known it was too late
for them because by then *Dead Ringer* was about to hit the
stands. But he had incautiously slept with her and they had
conceived Christina.

Not that Heddy told him about the baby. Nor had Jim
Bob gotten around to calling until the day Heddy was admitted to the hospital in premature labor. Leander had
rushed back to Kinney for what turned out to be the last
time. For two days he had paced the waiting room until
Christina was born.

When he had begged Tia to tell Heddy he was there and
that he wanted to see her, Tia had promised she would. A
few minutes later she had come out of Heddy's hospital
room and told him that Heddy, who had nearly died during
the difficult birth, didn't want to see him and that it would
be better for everybody if he didn't see the baby, either.

"All Heddy wants from you is a divorce," Tia had said
quietly. "And I don't blame her."

At the time, Leander had been staring out a window at the
pale flat prairie through the blinds and the stunted patches
of trees, at the land and sky that seemed to stretch forever,
thinking how this was the only place in the world that would
ever feel like home, thinking how Heddy was the only
woman he would ever love.

"Okay," he'd finally said in a weary voice. "I think you
know that I didn't kill Barret, but you win. I lose. If she

doesn't believe in me, our marriage is over. Tell her she can draw up the divorce papers."

Tia's eyes flashed with triumph. "How much will it cost me?"

"What?"

"How much will it cost me to be rid of you?"

"I don't want a dime."

"Of course you do. That's all your kind every wants."

"My kind?" His bitter voice had been edged with sarcasm. "Wrong. All I want is to get the hell out of here. Away from *your* kind. But . . . you'd damn sure better be good to Heddy and my daughter."

The funny thing was that Heddy had never asked him for a divorce.

Until Marcus.

High white clouds raced overhead. He glimpsed Orion again. Coyotes yelped at the moon and sent thin, quavering howls floating over the flat lonely land. A gust of cool damp air fanned Leander. The norther was due to hit any minute now.

With a polished shoe he kicked a rock into the dark ravine and heard the rapid scuttling of feet. Some varmint was prowling down there, probably an armadillo.

Leander thought of Heddy in her tight red sheath back in the ballroom dancing with Marcus. He kicked another rock over the edge and listened to it crash against brittle branches.

Damn it. He couldn't endure thoughts of that rich wimp pawing his wife.

Never had Leander felt sicker or tighter or more isolated. Not even in Alaska.

What he needed was a drink. And some company.

When he turned, he saw the brilliantly lit third story of the mansion hovering over the tops of the trees.

For him booze was always a dangerous mistake. It would be more so in some cheap beer joint in Kinney, Texas, with the locals after him.

But what the hell. He loped back toward the house in a dead run.

He needed a fight. A helluva lot more than he needed a drink.

And he found one, too. Right off—soon as he stepped into Rita's. Mac Benson, a former schoolyard bully, jumped him, shoving him drunkenly against the rough oak wall. Men were laughing and swearing, smoking and drinking. Not that he could see much in the gloom other than a tiny glittering Christmas tree over by the bar.

Not that Leander paid much attention to the bar's seedy ambience with Benson's brawny hand knotting the pleats of his dress shirt; with Benson's other fist aimed at his jaw.

Yeah, Leander would have had his fight. Only Mr. Q, the big bartender, decided to play vigilante. Mr. Q snapped the plug of the jukebox out of the wall, vaulted over the bar like a giant ape, and stuck his broken nose right in Mac's ugly potato white face even before Mac got through bellowing, "We don't want no truck here with no rich writer-murderer. You better git, Pepper—"

The crowd cheered Mac on drunkenly. "Get 'im, cowboy!"

"I'm the bouncer here, Mac. And I say you ride your horse off into the sunset. Knight stays." The silence in the bar was thick and hostile; everybody, even Mr. Q held his breath. "Or—you kin stay if you jest set yourself down again real friendlylike and shove that big nozzle of yours back in your own mug where it belongs, Mac."

The fickle crowd guffawed.

Somebody plugged in the jukebox. Music filled the room again, and everybody relaxed.

Mac flushed as Mr. Q methodically loosened Mac's black nailed fingers—one by one—from the ruined white pleats of Leander's shirt.

Leander swallowed, once he was free, and shrugged his wide shoulders so the wrinkles could fall out of the starched white cotton.

Mac wiped his forehead with the back of his hand. "You just got lucky, Pepper. But—"

"Anytime, Benson," Leander drawled nonchalantly. "And just so you know—I'm bunking in that old cabin out back of Jim Bob's."

"Maybe you think you're something 'cause you're rich and famous. But folks around here know who you really are, where you come from."

"Right."

As Mac sank grudgingly into a chair and lit a cigarette, Leander strode past him to the bar where he turned his broad, arrogant back on Mac and his sullen crowd in an attempt to ignore their glares and whispered jeers. Then he ordered a double Scotch on the rocks.

Mr. Q poured the whiskey very slowly. "A thank you would be nice, Pepper."

Leander bolted his whiskey—very fast. "I don't like people fighting my battles, Q," he muttered under his breath as he slid his empty shot glass toward the big man again.

"Then you shouldn't have come in here, Knight. I don't like fights."

Leander tapped the rim of his shot glass.

Q looked him in the eye as he poured. "Stay mellow, my friend."

Leander raised his hands innocently. "Hey—I'm not looking for trouble."

"Then why the hell did a famous writer like you come back to this one-horse hellhole when you know you ain't exactly the favorite hometown boy?"

The door opened as if in answer, and Q said, "Will you get a load of what the storm just blew in? It's your wife."

Leander turned and froze.

She might as well have been naked standing there with her red silk dress plastered wetly against her body.

Leander felt like he'd been hit by a cyclone. He sucked in a deep breath and then tossed down the second drink before he dared to look at Heddy again.

She was standing under the yellow neon glow of the beer sign, shivering and dripping water everywhere. Her damp hair spilled in wild tangles, long strands of it sticking to her bare shoulders. Her wet dress so transparent he could see her nipples. So could every other man in the bar.

When her soul-deep eyes zeroed in on Leander like radar, the blood rushed to his face.

She looked sexier than hell. And scared.

Almost as scared as he suddenly felt as he grabbed for the bottle of Scotch. With a shaking hand he made her a mocking salute. "You want to hear the joke of the century, Q? I came back because of her."

"Then you were damn sure lying when you said you weren't looking for trouble. 'Cause that's all that rich debutante's ever been to you."

"So, what else is new? Merry Christmas, Q." Leander took a lengthy pull from the bottle. "I was born on Christmas Eve. Did anybody ever tell you that? Same night she was. She used to say that meant she was my destiny. What kind of crazy sucker would fall for a corny line like that?"

Reflections from the Christmas lights gleamed in Q's steel gray eyes.

"You tell me—sucker."

Four

Churning fear. Heddy stared through the downpour at the bar. As one of Kinney's most respectable citizens, Heddy had driven past Rita's all her life without ever once considering going inside. The dive had an evil reputation and was frequented by border trash—smugglers, hard-drinking rednecks, and the lowest cowboys. The dearest tenet of their macho philosophy was that any woman dumb enough to come into Rita's was fair game.

Oh, God. Was she ever asking for it!

Tia would be furious if she ever found out that her granddaughter had gone inside such a place.

Heddy eyed Jim Bob's empty truck and then the squat frame building with the crooked line of Christmas lights dangling from its roofline and the tacky fake snowdrifts sprayed on its windowpanes. The jukebox was belting out hard rock so loudly she could feel the muted vibrations even in her Suburban with the windows rolled up and the rain streaming in torrents across her windshield.

She lowered her head and sagged against her steering wheel. All her life she had lived to please her family. An only, long-awaited child, their expectations, especially Tia's, had been so high for her. And she had failed them.

The sky went opalescent white and then inky black again. Flash; dark. Flash; dark, blinding her, causing her heart to race and her breath to quicken as she reconsidered her options.

Maybe she shouldn't have been so fast to abandon Marcus on the ballroom dance floor and follow Leander into Kinney. But when she had seen him coming from the path that led to the ravine, looking so dark and tormented, it had seemed imperative to follow him.

She'd been so miserable dancing with Marcus. There had been no magic in his cool, light touch. No soul-deep fire in his gentle brown eyes. She liked him. But only as a friend. Which wasn't nearly enough after Leander.

Suddenly Heddy had been unable to continue the charade—even for Tia, who'd been watching them. Heddy had made some excuse to Marcus and run outside.

Maybe she could have fallen in love with Marcus if Leander hadn't come back and held her in his arms and kissed her. If she hadn't seen how wonderful he was with Christina.

But it was too late now.

Leander had come home, and nothing would ever be the same for her again. She was no longer a child, no longer so easily led in her thinking by older people.

Leander had always said he was innocent.

She remembered how he'd always avoided fighting with her father. How he'd begged her to believe him. How he'd always faithfully sent generous support payments for

Christina and demanded nothing in return. People had called him a gold digger. But the truth was he'd been prouder than any Kinney when it came to money. He'd worked hard for the ranch when they'd been married. After their separation, he'd never taken a dime. And now he was a wealthy man in his own right.

Why had Leander come back when it would have been so much simpler for him to divorce her? Why had he kissed her with such tenderness and passion, as if he cared for her with every atom of his being?

Then, later that night, just when she'd been crazy from thinking about him, he had burst out of the stunted trees with the look of a man chased by demons from hell.

She had known that path. Where it led. Where he'd been.

Suddenly she had wanted to discover the truth. About her father and about Leander's true feelings. About her own.

Just as she'd climbed into her Suburban to follow him, the norther had blown in with gusting winds and big drops splashing and starring her windshield. Once she'd caught up to him, she'd kept his bobbing taillights in sight until he'd veered from the highway into Rita's. She'd hit her brakes and U-turned it, her tires skidding off the shoulder and howling. She'd parked between his empty, mud-spattered truck and two big black motorcycles.

As she sagged wearily against her steering wheel, the canvas awning over the front door shredded in the wind.

Don't go in, a silent voice warned. *They'll tear you apart.*

Afraid she'd lose her nerve, she slung open her heavy car door into the wind. Her sodden skirts were plastered to her legs even before she reached the entrance.

Music and smoke and men's laughter and drunken wolf whistles blasted her the minute she stepped inside.

"Sit here, baby," yelled a florid-faced biker in black leather.

"No, over here, sexy."

The smoky bar was so dark, she couldn't see. But she had the impression of several men in black leather crowded around small tables, drinking and smoking, swearing and shouting to be heard over the blasting music. There were half a dozen kickers in sweat-stained Stetsons at another table.

Then a Texas-sized barrel of a man with a fat potato face and a straw Stetson shoved a chair back and staggered toward her, his hot, narrowed eyes too interested. She caught a whiff of beer on his breath as he reached her.

She *had* to find Leander. *Fast*.

"Well, well. Just look what the cat dragged in," a familiar voice said suggestively against her ear.

"Hi, Mac," she breathed, relaxing a little since she knew him.

"Hi, back," he said, leaning closer, his eyes on her breasts instead of her face. "Thought you was having a big old party out at the ranch."

"It's still going on."

"But you came looking for a crowd that's more fun?"

"Not exactly, Mac."

Her eyes had grown accustomed to the smoke-filled gloom. She scanned the nearby tables first. Then the rest of the bar.

She was near panic when suddenly she recognized Leander's crisp crop of black hair and his tall, linebacker's physique across the room near the Christmas tree. He had stripped out of his tuxedo jacket and was hunched over the bar. His pleated white shirt was unbuttoned at the collar and rolled up to his elbows, revealing tanned, muscular forearms.

"I—I was looking for my husband."

Desperate to attract Leander's attention, she raised her hand to wave at him.

Mac grabbed it, crushing the bones of her wrist, stepping between her and the bar, blocking her view of her husband before Leander could notice her.

"Let me go, Mac. Please—"

Reluctantly the big man obeyed. But the minute she pulled free, he leaned toward her again, and with a lewd gesture, used his thick middle finger to unstick a tendril of wet hair from her cheek. "Now ain't that too bad. The rain done messed up your hairdo. I was just saying what a damn shame it is for a pretty little thing like yourself to be mixed up with a nut case like Pepper, who shot your daddy and then got rich bragging about it in a novel."

She pushed his big hand away. "Nobody ever proved that."

"'Cause y'all covered for him. Maybe it's about time we got some real justice around here."

Leander had looked up and was watching her now. She waved at him, and he saluted her by tipping his liquor bottle ever so slightly.

"Y'all leave him alone, Mac," she pleaded before turning and heading toward the bar.

Wolf whistles and hot stares followed her the entire way.

Leander watched her, too, but in a nicer way that caused every nerve in her body to prickle pleasantly.

"You look a little breathless, Sugar. And you damn sure know how to stir up a ruckus," he said edgily, pulling a stool out for her. "Why don't you sit down and put on my coat?"

He leaned toward her and picked up his jacket.

His white shirt was unbuttoned halfway down his bronzed chest. She remembered how hot he always got when he wore a coat or tie, how anxious he always was to strip out of them. He smiled, a slow lazy smile that transformed his carved features.

Her throat tightened. He seemed so primitively male, so powerful and dangerous—so sinfully handsome.

"I wanted to talk to you," she whispered.

Leander was studying her intently, too, as he draped his coat over her shoulders. When he was done, he took another long pull from his bottle. Then he hooked his other wrist casually and yet possessively over the backrest of her stool. "You should have caught me before I started drinking. I'm too far gone to think. Much less talk."

"Maybe you should slow it down," she said.

"Maybe." With a mocking grin he took another pull.

She watched his lips on the rim of the bottle. When she caught a glimpse of his tongue, unwanted heat climbed her neck.

Nearby someone muttered, "You wouldn't think she'd have anything to do with a loony who killed her father."

Leander's jaw tightened. With an effort he kept his tone casual. "What the hell do you think you're doing—coming here?"

"What will you have, little lady?" Mr. Q interrupted.

"Nothing." Leander's whisper was suddenly tense. "She's leaving."

"Whatever he's drinking," Heddy countered, pulling the black jacket closer around herself. "I'm staying."

Mr. Q pitched three ice cubes in a glass. Then he grabbed Leander's bottle. "Double Scotch on the rocks for the little lady."

"Thanks, Q. I'm *very* thirsty." Her sip began nonchalantly enough. But when the Scotch scalded her throat, she suddenly lurched forward, sputtering and gagging. Leander patted her on the back. She would have taken another sip if Leander's long fingers hadn't curved around her glass.

"Easy does it, Sugar. Maybe you should slow it down."

At the rasping brush of his fingers, she spilled her drink all over the counter.

A hostile murmur went through the crowd as Mr. Q mopped it up with a towel.

"You're attracting attention again," Leander said, a warning in his low tone.

She pulled her glass free of his grip and lifted it to her lips again. "So? Maybe I was trying to."

"I don't like it. You're making them madder. Mac and those jerks are staring at you. You shouldn't have come in here."

"Neither should you. But we're here, aren't we? Together. The question is—what are we going to do about it?"

"I think you should get the hell out of here before this place blows like a keg of dynamite," he said.

"Maybe I feel more like a party." His coat slid off her shoulders as she picked up one of the quarters he'd left on the bar for a tip and handed it to Mr. Q. "Play something we can dance to. Something slow. Something country. Better yet—" She leaned forward and whispered a specific title into Mr. Q's ear before she turned back to Leander. "I want to finish what we started."

"What was that?"

"We were dancing. Remember?"

The music started—slow, twangy—country, but with a heavy beat. She looked everywhere except at him. His bronzed masculinity was evoking a pagan response. Her senses were fighting a losing battle against the desire to be crushed against the muscular strength of his chest.

She slanted her eyes to him. "Well, what do you know?" she said silkily. "They're playing our old song."

Behind the bar, the lights of the Christmas tree winked at her. For a long moment the years slid away and they were young and in love.

He was staring into her eyes, forgetting himself. Then his black gaze left her face and roamed over the shapely length of her body as if he, too, found her irresistible. "That's one helluva dress," he muttered. "You'd better put my damned jacket back on."

"I'm glad you like it," she said without pretense... without reserve.

"That's not what I said. I said put—"

When she tentatively put her hand on the white cotton covering his broad shoulder, one of his nerves jumped. His incredible body heat seeped through his damp sleeve into her fingertips. "Dance with me," she whispered, leaning so close that her breath beat upon his face. "For old time's sake."

One minute stretched into two.

"No way, Sugar," he finally said, jerking away from her touch. "Not here. Not to that song."

She lifted her head and their eyes held again. "Then somewhere private."

"Look, Sugar. You were right. I was wrong. I shouldn't have come back. Nothing's changed except my hide isn't as thick as it used to be. I don't like people thinking I'm this weirdo writer who killed Barret when I didn't. I especially don't like you thinking it. I'll give you your divorce whenever you want it. It'll be my Christmas present."

She swayed even closer. "You didn't used to be such a coward, Leander Knight."

"I was too damn dumb to know to be scared."

When she touched him again, he shot off his stool like her hand burned him, the same as his heat burned her.

"I don't want a divorce for Christmas, any more than you do," she whispered fiercely.

He grabbed her wrist. "Look—don't come on to me. I don't like to be teased."

Her seductive glance flitted to the sensual line of his lips. She ached to feel his mouth on hers, to know that she inflamed him as he did her. "Leander," she said simply. "I'm not teasing."

He let her go and threw down a twenty-dollar bill.

When he slammed his stool back under the bar and strode toward the door, she raced after him.

He plunged out into the thick sheets of rain.

So did she.

When he hopped in his truck and locked the door, she beat on his window in frustration as the thick, cold rain blasted her.

He took his time lowering the glass. "You're getting drenched. Give it up, Sugar." As he backed out slowly, careful not to hurt her, she banged on the side of his truck with her open palms.

He waved goodbye as he revved the engine, his tires spinning gravel and pellets against her bare legs as he kept backing.

The rain was thicker than ever, colder. She'd left his jacket inside and was soon so thoroughly soaked, she was shivering. As he pulled out onto the highway, she got in her Suburban, scooped her keys off the floorboard and sped after him.

Not that he made it easy for her. By the time she swerved onto the highway, his truck had vanished.

She floored the Suburban, her transmission screaming. And a few seconds later she saw the red glare of his brake lights as he swerved too fast to the left off the main road.

His tires hit fresh gravel. She held her breath when his truck slewed violently. Geysers of water shot from his back wheels as his vehicle skidded off the road.

Oh, no… She eased off her accelerator and took the turn slowly, carefully pulling up on the shoulder behind him.

She flashed her headlights on and off.

Ignoring her, he restarted Jim Bob's truck. His engine roared, but his right wheels spun uselessly in the mud.

She laughed.

She had him now.

After two jaunty toots of her horn he didn't get out, so she jumped out into the icy deluge.

When she banged on his window, she saw he was on his car phone. He stared down at her. For a second she thought he was going to stay where he was. Then he cut his engine and threw open his door.

Very slowly he got out, too.

"You should be glad I'm here to rescue you," she said almost lightly.

His mouth was set in a straight line, his eyes dark and empty before her words relit that swift light of anger in his face. "I told you to go home, Sugar."

"You used to drive better than that," she mocked.

He caught her arm and slammed her against his truck. "You didn't used to chase me so hard."

"You never ran," she said.

His savage gaze glittered. "I wasn't on to you, back then."

"I don't think you really feel like running tonight," she said.

There was the barest tightening to his jaw. He might have argued that point, too, but she kissed him.

Lips against lips. Although the contact was brief, it set her pulse racing.

"You're wrong, baby," he muttered, jerking away. But even as his words defied her, his gaze was dwelling on her mouth as if he couldn't forget the taste of her.

Her arms went around his lean waist, her fingers splaying as she drew him toward her. "I don't think so, Leander."

The rain was cold as it blasted them, trickling through their hair, down their spines in icy rivulets, plastering their clothes to their bodies.

But his reluctant lips were hot when he forcefully caught the back of her neck with his hand and, tilting her face, lowered his mouth to hers. His tongue was hot, too, when it invaded her lips and filled her mouth. His arms tightened around her like steel bands as he shoved her against his truck.

She gasped at the sudden heated contact with the rock wall of his chest. For a long moment his mouth smothered hers, and she couldn't breathe. She saw a thousand pin pricks of brilliance behind her closed eyes before blackness swirled around her.

"Ah, Heddy—" he groaned. "I swore I'd never let this happen again."

She caught her breath and sighed as she looked at the rough carving of his dark features. "Me, too."

The icy rain beat down. She was standing ankle-deep in a frigid puddle. Every time she moved, water sloshed inside her sodden designer shoes. But she didn't care.

His warm hand was suddenly on her breast, kneading her warm flesh through the wet transparent silk. Her nipple was swelling and hardening against his palm. She'd never felt so hot, so purely a creature of animal instinct, her body open and quivering with wonderful, glorious, burning needs.

"I'm not running now—though God knows I should," he whispered, still kissing her, his arms locked around her in a

tranglehold of desire as he picked her up and carried her to
her Suburban. "What do you say we get the hell out of
here?"

Inside her car he placed her across the back seat and de-
oured her mouth hungrily for a long moment. His deep-
ning kisses touched off the passionate core of her body and
et her on fire. When he began lifting wet silk out of the way
and touching her intimately, her icy skin turned to flame.
Not once did she try to stop his roaming hands as he molded
her curves to the hard contours of his male length.

Another car swept past, showering the Suburban with a
wave of water and gravel and brilliant headlights.

His voice was husky as he lifted his mouth from the
warmth of her throat. "What the hell are we doing, Sugar?
Making love in the backseat of your car like teenagers when
anybody might drive up?"

On a harsh shudder he let her go. Draping a long arm over
the front seat, he jingled the keys in her ignition.

"Climb on over, Sugar," he ordered softly.

Pulling herself up on her elbows, she stared at him daz-
edly.

"You'd better drive. You've had a helluva lot less than
I've had to drink." He spoke in an offhand manner. "I'm
staying in that old cabin behind the Janovich place."

"What?"

Another car rushed by peppering them with gravel and
brushing them with a brilliant arc of white light again.

In the darkness that followed, she wished he would touch
her or hold her, that he would show some small sign of tenderness or affection. But he was frowning. His dark face was
harsh; his smooth tone too cynical. "I'm asking you to
spend the night with me. No strings attached."

She felt an empty ache in the pit of her stomach.

"I want to sleep with you, Sugar. Don't look so shocked. That's why you came on to me in the bar, wasn't it?"

When she turned her back to him, he yanked her around and kissed her again. His kiss was lush, intimate, from the moment his mouth covered hers.

He tasted of Scotch whiskey and sublime temptation.

"I may not be good enough to be your husband. You might even believe me capable of murder. But you still want me in your bed, don't you? And I'm so desperate for any scrap of affection—I'll take what I can get."

Murder? She had forgotten all that. For a numbed moment she cringed as she guiltily remembered her father.

Leander's black eyes blazed darkly. His wet hair was plastered against his inky brows. His chiseled features were etched with the harsh determination to have his way no matter what.

Was he guilty? Or innocent?

In that moment he seemed so hard. When she scooted away from him, recoiling from the ruthlessness she saw in him, his lips thinned.

"You put me in hell, too, Sugar," he whispered, seething. "For years I was the poor boy bastard your family said wasn't good enough for their rich, blue-blooded princess. Then you and the gossips of this little burg convicted me on a rumor for a murder I didn't commit. I've tried to hate you. I buried myself alive. But you haunted me. No matter how hard I tried to forget you, I couldn't. As for Marcus—" Leander's curt voice broke abruptly as his arms tightened around her. "Tonight, you're mine."

Five

Leander felt like he was coiled tighter than a spring as he stood beside Heddy's stiff figure and fumbled for his key.

"Damn it, I said I was sorry," he whispered.

"Right. Technically I suppose you did."

"What more do you want?"

"Oh—nothing. Or... or maybe just for you to mean it."

More silence. From her.

From him, too.

"You just don't get it. Like I'm really sorry that it gets to me that you desire me even though you still think I'm a killer."

As he shoved the door open, he pitched his key ring past her, scarcely noting in his frustration that it fell between his suitcase and his laptop computer. She stepped inside hesitantly, freezing when she saw the bed. He stopped, too, suddenly seeing his drab room through her aristocratic eyes.

The cabin had ancient cowhide lamp shades with scorc
marks. A wagon wheel with deer antlers and little lamp
swung over the dining room table at a cockeyed angle. A
threadbare Indian blanket had been thrown across his bed

"Sorry...about the cabin, Sugar. You're used to a whol
lot better—"

"No—I was remembering how it was when we came her
as kids. You were so messy then. But I loved coming here
being alone with you." Her voice had softened. Some of th
strain had left her white face.

"You were sweet to me back then. At least most of th
time."

"Life seemed so simple then," she agreed.

Flushing, he pivoted abruptly. His heels made hollow
sounds on the scuffed oak floor as he walked over to th
pine dresser. There he pulled open a drawer so that she coul
see it contained plenty of blankets that they could use t
wrap up in after they'd stripped out of their wet clothes.

She didn't smile or even look at him as she took a blu
one. "Everything's happened so fast. I don't know what t
think, Leander."

For a long moment there were only the sounds of hi
magnified heartbeats and their breaths.

"You could give me the benefit of the doubt, for
change."

She squeezed her eyes shut and nodded. "I am trying to."

"Hey," he murmured. "I'm sorry I yelled at you." Whe
she turned away, his arms went around her in a vise. Hi
hand pressed her golden head against his chest, holding he
possessively against him. "But this is hard for me, too," h
said gently, lowering his lips to her throat, nibbling until he
heartbeat skittered madly. A wild peace enveloped them fo
an endless time.

She turned to face him, placing her cold hands against his warm cheeks. "Why are you always so hot?"

"High metabolism. I eat a lot. Remember how you used to steal food off my plate."

Her lips parted. "You never minded."

"I used to wish so hard that I'd been born rich or even born legitimate—just so your family would approve of me. Why would I care if you stole my food? I always wanted to give you the world, Heddy." With heated fingertips he tilted her chin up and stared at her. "I didn't kill your father. I would never hurt anyone you loved."

She was silent. And beautiful. So beautiful with her luminous, sapphire eyes, with her long, inky lashes and her slanting brows. Her delectable mouth was gently curved, her nose straight and finely boned. Her breasts rose and fell as she breathed in and out. She was both innocent and voluptuously sensual. He could hardly think, so powerfully was he attracted to her.

But she didn't believe him.

Which was the reason he'd left her and stayed away and sworn never to come back.

He had two choices—to drive her home or to take her to bed.

Her lush mouth parted again, and she moistened her lips with her tongue. The shattering kisses in her Suburban came back to torment him.

Hell. For eight years he'd dreamed of that mouth, of her body. Of her.

There was no choice. He was too far gone to let her go— no matter what she thought of him. No way could he face the bitter loneliness of Jim Bob's cabin without her. If he didn't take her, he'd torture himself for the rest of his life with the fantasy of what he'd passed up.

Leander knew he was going to kiss her, and there wasn't a damn thing he could do about it.

And the instant his mouth brushed her upper lip and her fingers curled tighter into his chest, he knew that this kiss was like none of the others because they both knew where it would end.

His mouth was tender and yet eager. He didn't rush—it was a kiss of considerable restraint and yet of deep hunger.

When she opened her mouth to accept his tongue, he knew a soul-jolting thrill.

"You'd better take off that wet dress," he said, after the first taste of her tongue and teeth started his heart beating too fast. He sucked in a gulp of air. "Before you catch your death—"

"I don't care, Leander."

"I do," he muttered hoarsely.

Breaking free, she tiptoed with elfin grace to the bathroom.

While she undressed in his tiny bathroom, Leander phoned a cousin of Jim Bob's who had a tow truck and asked him to pick up his truck on the side of the road. Then he stacked logs and lit a fire in the fireplace, so that the room was aglow with a rosy warmth when she came out bundled in the soft blue blanket. He was still so worked up from their kiss that when she accidentally gave him an eyeful of long shapely leg as she settled down by the fire, he craved nothing more than a session of hot, dangerous, all-or-nothing sex. Yet, he was afraid of sex with her. He was afraid it would suck him in too deep.

She didn't help much when she looked up at him dreamily, her eyes pulling him into her in that soul-deep way, like blue magnets. "Why don't you get out of those wet clothes and come sit by the fire?"

"Hey, that's supposed to be my line."

"I'm already undressed." Her damp shoulders were bare. Her wet hair slicked back. She looked young and vulnerable and sexily wanton. "Take your clothes off."

"Good idea," he rasped. "But—"

She felt his hesitation. "Leander, I'm still your wife."

"Technically maybe. But we've been separated more years than we lived together."

Her lovely eyes shimmered with loneliness. And with desire. "I never slept with anybody else. Does that count?"

Yeah. It counted. Too much.

"We still have a very complicated relationship. There's Christina. And Tia."

"Leander, is there . . . is there somebody else?"

"Hell, there's the whole damned town." He paused. "For the record—I haven't slept with anybody for a long time, either," he breathed.

Her sudden smile was radiant. "Good."

Why the hell had he admitted that? "Not that it's any of your business."

She smiled again when he reddened. "Go take a hot shower. And hurry back. I'm already feeling lonesome."

He took his time. Not that it mattered. As soon as he returned and hunkered down by the fire, she was all over him, snuggling close, smelling fresh and clean and feminine.

"Women are always after you. Are you telling me the truth about your not sleeping—"

He flushed darkly. "I wouldn't make too much of it if I were you. There aren't enough women in Alaska to go around. Especially on the island."

"If you had wanted another woman, you'd have had one." She touched his tanned face, traced the line of his jaw, the hollow of his throat, not saying anything more. She didn't have to. Her eyes spoke volumes. So did the magic fingertips that fired his warm skin.

He could see that she wanted him. Every bit as much as he wanted her. And suddenly nothing else mattered.

She kissed him, her firm lips warm and light in the beginning, but things heated up fast. Within seconds they were stretched length to length, and he was breathing as hard as a marathon runner. He was soon so hot he was peeling off their blankets. Hers first, unwrapping her gorgeous body as if she were a priceless Christmas present, tracing the curves of her exquisite breasts with his palms until she made small gasping sounds of pleasure.

"Heddy—"

"Relax," she whispered, placing his hands back on her creamy flesh, running her own fingers over his hair-roughened arms and torso.

Her skin felt as smooth as satin. Her wet golden hair streamed out over the blue blanket and oak floor in silken waves as she lay back, guiding him toward her, letting his hands move between her thighs, touching first all the allowable spots before those crying out to be touched.

She pulled his blanket off, too, kissing his dark body, his wide shoulders, his taut stomach and sinewy muscles. Her hands followed the path of her lips, stroking lower, down the length of his abdomen, as if she were polishing a living bronze statue. And then finding his manhood, her fingers circled it, sliding back and forth until he groaned aloud.

A few minutes later he jerked away from her. For a second or two she whimpered while he fumbled with a box in the darkness.

"Leander?"

He held up the box of condoms so she could see what he was doing. When he had one on, he rolled back over and feathered her damp brow with kisses. With a silent moan of helpless surrender, she arched her body up to meet his.

He murmured an inarticulate sound of passion. Then with a single thrust he was inside her, binding them body and soul, whispering her name as he tenderly kissed her lips and throat. He began rocking back and forth, driving ever deeper, giving himself shatteringly to the ardent task of satisfying her. Her fingertips tunneled into his black hair. She was whispering his name, clinging, sighing, pleading.

As always, her body was a perfect fit. As always, she excited him as no other woman could, drawing him out of the lonely depths of his solitude. His breath grew heavier as his fever for her rose. And soon, sooner than either of them wanted, swift, hot waves of carnal excitement were sweeping them both to dizzying heights that were greater than they'd ever known.

His head came up in that last moment, and he looked into her unwavering jewel-dark eyes. Tilting her head back, he fused their mouths, his lips grinding against hers, his tongue mating with hers.

He was out of control.

So was she.

And when she found shattering ecstasy, she sent him spiraling over the edge, too.

For a long time after their shared bliss, he lay on top of her, crushing her damp body beneath his. For a timeless moment all their tensions were suspended, and he savored the comfort of her warmth and nearness.

Only she could repel the darkness inside him. The loneliness and pain of the past, all that stood between them, dissolved in that moment of blistering glory.

She was all that had ever mattered to him.

When they were children she had diminished the agony of his lonely childhood, just by being there. Before her he had felt that he was less than nothing because his own mother had thrown him away. Then Heddy had befriended him and made other children befriend him. Because she had believed in him, he had started believing in himself. All that he had ever accomplished was due to her. That was why her betrayal had hurt worse than anything in his whole life.

Outside the wind and rain raged. Inside the fire died down and they lay together in secret, loving peace. He fell asleep still holding her, clinging to the fragile dream that he hadn't come this far to lose her again.

And then the telephone rang.

Dimly he felt Heddy's warm body untangling from his as she reached an arm lazily across his chest to lift the receiver.

Leander's stomach tightened at the instant guilt in Heddy's muted voice when she said, "Tia!"

His eyes opened. As he studied the ceiling, his temples began to pound—from the Scotch, from the long airplane flights, from the sex—or maybe just from listening to the strain in Heddy's voice.

Shapes lit by the dying embers of the fire came slowly into focus. He made out the hideous antler chandelier, the gleam of Heddy's tangled hair. Most of all he felt the heaviness of Tia's spirit coming between them again.

"It just happened, Tia. He ran Jim Bob's truck off the road," Heddy was saying in that hollow tone he hated. "I couldn't very well just leave him there when it was pouring."

Leander's opaque eyes glittered in the dark. "Why don't you tell her you were chasing me when I ran off the road, Sugar?"

With a shudder Heddy clamped her hand over the receiver. "Hush." She removed her fingers, one by one. "I—I don't know, Tia. I—I just felt like a drive."

"Sugar, why don't you tell her how you were feeling when you came on to me in the bar in that wet, skin-tight, see-through red dress—"

"Mac called?" Heddy said sharply, whitening. "Yes, I did go there." Her remorseful voice was nearly inaudible. "I know. It was kind of a crazy thing to do."

"Not any crazier than coming here, Sugar. Not any crazier than...this." Leander's hand moved under the sheets and ran up her silky, naked thigh.

She jumped away from his heated fingers with a startled cry. "No, Tia. It was nothing. I—I just...saw a mouse. I'm okay. I—I swear."

Heddy hung up and sank stiffly against her pillow. When he started to roll on top of her, she backed away. "I have to go."

"Heddy—" He ached to hold her again, to know the warm bliss of her body in the darkness again. But instead of reaching for her, he got defensive, too, which made him retreat into that place deep inside himself that was like a frozen ice cave where he could shut out everyone who rejected him, even her. He found angry words and forced them out.

"Right," he began. "Tia called. And she doesn't like it that you're with me. So, what's new? You're torn between the two of us again. And you'll choose her because you always do. But before you go, could you forget Tia and tell me what you feel about what happened here tonight?"

Heddy's pale expression was unreadable. "Tia wants to know why. She wants to know how—how I could be here with you. I guess maybe I do, too."

"You tell me, Heddy. You followed me to that bar. You asked me to dance. You kissed me in the rain. Did you want sex? Or did you want something more?"

Heddy sprang off the bed. Then realizing she was naked, she yanked the sheet off him and wrapped it around herself.

His muscular body lay sprawled across the bed without a stitch on. "What gets you hot, Heddy? My bad reputation . . . or me?"

"Shut up," she whispered, dragging her gaze from him with an immodest reluctance that fired his blood. "Just shut up. This isn't helping." Her voice was quavering with anger.

"Are you mad because you like sleeping with me? Or because Tia has you back to thinking I murdered Barret?"

She compressed her lips and turned away again. He watched her, wanting to push her even harder and demand answers.

She whisked her dress off the chair by the fire. When she disappeared into his bathroom, he got up.

Seething, he yanked clothes off hangers in his closet, pulling on his jeans and a Western shirt. Then he rummaged on his closet floor for his belt and boots.

When she came out of the bathroom, he was grabbing his black Stetson hat from a peg on the wall by the door.

She stared at him, her anguished face darkening with embarrassment as she realized his intention. "Where do you think you're going?"

"I'm driving you home, Sugar."

"Not in my car. We can't be seen—"

"Together?" he mocked, finishing her thought. "By Tia or somebody else? You ashamed of me, like before?" He felt a muscle ticking savagely in his neck.

She blushed, equally furious. "Yes! Yes! I'm embarrassed they'll know—" Her eyes darted to the tangled white sheets and Indian blanket on his bed.

"Sugar, it's a little late to worry on that score. Tia already knows about us, and the whole town'll know tomorrow you chased me out of the bar. I don't want you out this late alone. You could have an accident. Somebody might chase you and run you off the road. I don't want just anybody... rescuing you."

She stood stock-still, her eyes wide as he leaned down and scooped up his keys.

"Leander, I hate this as much as you do."

He let a moment of silence pass. "Somehow I doubt that."

"But if—if you didn't kill my father, who did? Is it so terrible that—that I just want to know what really happened to him?"

All the warmth he'd felt for her congealed. He hated her thinking him that low. And because his own emotions were so ravaged, because he had retreated into that dark cold part of himself, his voice came out harsh and razor sharp with sarcasm.

"Don't we all, Sugar. But what I wanted more than that was for you to believe in me. You don't. You won't ever. Which means our marriage is over. What galls me the most is that I still give a damn. But for the record—I don't intend to for long."

He strode toward the door and shoved it open for her. When she stayed where she was, he stepped quietly outside into the wet, wild night without her.

Some instinct warned him of the danger.

He heard shouts. Then flashlights blinded him.

There was a deafening shotgun blast. Another gunshot.

"Don't come out!" he yelled, reeling backward as a steel bullet creased his temple, snapping his black hat off. Blood spurted from his hair and streamed into his eyes.

"Got the creepy bastard," someone screamed.

Blinded by blood and the darkness after the flashlights, Leander crawled back inside, shouting hoarsely to Heddy to get down. When she didn't obey instantly, he grabbed her ankle and pulled her beneath him, blanketing her with his own body.

There was a final shotgun blast as he kicked the door shut. As they lay in the darkness, his larger body almost completely smothering hers, he heard racing footsteps outside, shouts, and a truck engine and a motorcycle roared to life.

Still shielding Heddy, he dragged her to the window and cautiously watched a late-model sedan and a big motorcycle race away in the wet darkness.

When his assailants were gone, Leander slumped against the wall, all his emotions draining out of him as his blood dripped from his brow onto the carpet. He felt dizzy, sick. He saw Heddy's face, heard her frantic whispers before he lost consciousness.

When he gradually came to a few seconds later, his head hurting like it was going to split in two, Heddy was kneeling beside him, bathing his face with a cold towel.

"I think it's just a nick," she said soothingly.

He heard her through a mist of pain and nausea.

When her wet rag stung him again, he grabbed her wrist and opened his eyes. "Just a nick?" he howled fiercely.

"A scratch," she confirmed, her tone gentle. "Did...did you see who shot you?"

He touched his hand to his face and found only a trace of sticky blood.

"No. It could have been anybody."

He lay back, relaxing, his anger for the moment gone, not caring if the whole town wanted him dead if she cared this much, liking her gentle fingers smoothing his black hair away from his brow so that she could apply the gauze dressing.

When he winced, she murmured anxiously, "Are you okay? I—I don't like hurting you."

"Yeah. Right." The constriction in his throat made his deep voice sound weak.

Her pale face grew very remorseful. Her lips bent to kiss the bandage. "No, I don't. I really don't like hurting you," she repeated dully.

"Then it was almost worth getting shot up," he said. "To know you care, even if you don't believe—"

When her fingertips stroked his rough cheeks, his heart began to pound.

Her dark lashes fluttered. "I care," she whispered. "Too much."

"It always was fun—making up after one of our fights."

"Yes, it was."

"Heddy," he said hoarsely. "Do you ever think— Do you ever hope that—"

He stopped himself and wearily closed his eyes. For years he'd schooled himself not to dream the impossible.

For a long moment it was enough that they could share the darkness together, that they could find comfort if not peace once more in each other's company.

When the phone rang again, he knew even before Heddy picked it up that it would be Tia.

Six

Wind lashed the palm fronds in front of the big house, but the fury of the storm was nothing compared to the turmoil Tia felt as she stood in the arched doorway and watched the rain batter the thick palms in the middle of her circular drive.

As always her annual Christmas party had been a huge success, the last of her glittering guests having been whisked away by limousine to the airport hours ago. But Tia was not thinking with either pleasure or pride of the ball she had carefully orchestrated.

Her aristocratic features were set in an icy mask. Every time Tia remembered Heddy abandoning Marcus on the dance floor and running after Leander, her heart rushed with an odd pain that took her breath away. She felt weak and old—and very ill equipped to deal with her impossible grandson-in-law.

But she had to fight him one last time.

Tia had sensed he'd be trouble when Heddy had rushed home from school and told her about the poor boy she'd saved from a fight. The minute Tia had seen him, she'd known at once he was a cocky, self-serving upstart who had befriended Heddy solely because he was impressed with her money and position. Later he had married her for the same reason and had used the scandal and tragedy following Barret's death to promote himself into a world-famous writer.

Tia remembered the first afternoon Heddy had brought him home. He'd been a skinny ten-year-old with holes in his jeans. Tia had hidden on the second-floor landing and observed him. His black eyes had gleamed as he'd stared at the black-and-white marble floors in the foyer, the three-story spiral staircase and the enormous chandelier that hung in the foyer.

Tia remembered Heddy's almost feverish excitement as she had dashed about, letting him turn the chandelier on and off, letting him handle all the house's treasures. He had been clumsy and self-conscious, not wanting to touch anything, but Heddy had made him.

How Tia had relished his terror when he and Heddy had dropped a priceless Dresden porcelain figurine. He had wanted to confess at once, swearing he'd work for her grandmother forever to pay for it, but Heddy had insisted on hiding the broken bits under a table—an action that had proved to Tia the boy was a corrupting influence.

Tia had swept down the stairs then, pretending to know nothing of the Dresden figure, inviting the scarlet-faced children to tea and cookies on the terrace, only noting the absence of the figurine after she had lulled him into a false sense of security.

When they were once more in the foyer and she was showing him out, she had innocently commented that the

Dresden piece wasn't there. He'd flushed as Tia had pretended to search the china closets. Tia had been haughtily magnanimous when he'd confessed and shown her where the broken fragments were. She had soothed the embarrassed boy. At the same time she had let him know how irreplaceable the figurine was. She had made him see that he shouldn't play with things he couldn't afford. Secretly she had hoped to make him feel so outclassed and uncomfortable that he would realize he didn't belong and would never return.

And he never had come into their house again until that disastrous day when he'd returned as Heddy's husband. Tia remembered how happy the young couple had been, how full of young love and hope. When Tia had greeted them coldly, Pepper had sworn that he knew he wasn't good enough for Heddy in her eyes, but if she'd just give him a chance, she'd soon see that no man could ever love her granddaughter as he did.

Not that either she or Barret had believed him. From the first, Tia had been determined to find some way to break them up. And since she had known Heddy so well, she had known just how to manipulate events to diminish Pepper in her eyes. How Tia had loved having the kind of parties and inviting snobs she'd been sure would ask the kinds of questions that most embarrassed and infuriated him. She had used pretended kindness to destroy him.

And now the bastard was back.

When Tia saw the arc of white headlights at the gate, her heart jerked painfully again and began palpitating with sharp fits and starts when she got a glimpse of the tall man in the Stetson beside Heddy.

Tall and lean, still the rangy cowboy, Leander jumped out of the Suburban and helped Heddy down. Tia hated the way he bent his dark bandaged head so attentively to Heddy's, the way she smiled so sweetly up at him as they joined hands and ran together through the rain toward the house.

The disgusting display of affection between them could mean only one thing—that Heddy had given into the wild, headstrong part of her nature that had been such a problem when she'd been a girl. She had slept with him again.

Thinking themselves alone, the lovers melted together under the awning, their mouths clinging for an endless time before reluctantly breaking apart. Tia's hand went to her chest. Her eyes grew as hard as stones as Heddy touched the white bandage at his temple and smoothed the damp lock of black hair that was falling carelessly across his forehead.

They were more in love than ever.

The storm door whined as Tia pushed it ajar and stepped out of the darkness, her intent to drive him away.

The wind was like a physical blow, banging the door back into the stucco wall and unbalancing her so that she teetered as rain blasted her.

Odd—how the cold air made her heart tighten and turned the joints of her knees to jelly, how her old eyes had trouble focusing on Heddy and Leander, who were now peering up at her.

"Tia?" Leander demanded.

The bruised center of her chest tightened again, this time radiating sharp, paralyzing wavelets of pain. When she tried to catch a breath, she couldn't.

"Tia, I didn't see you there," Heddy began in a frightened rush. "Is anything the matter?"

Tia clutched her chest, gasping for air. Heddy's lovely face began to swim in a sea of raindrops and darkness as she fought to speak.

An iron band wound around Tia's chest, crushing her diaphragm so tightly she couldn't breathe.

Her heart was beating violently now; her gown was wet with perspiration. And she felt heavy. Too heavy to stand.

"Dizzy," she said in a weak, baffled voice as her knees buckled and she grabbed for the railing.

As the polished wood slipped from her grasp and she staggered, Leander plunged toward her through the darkness.

Their eyes locked.

His expression was kind, almost gentle; hers aflame with implacable hatred. Even so it was she who recoiled.

"No—" She pushed herself away from him, stumbling backward.

In terror of him.

Her mouth went dry as he caught her, cradling her gently as he lowered her to the ground.

"Tia, Tia—" Heddy was sobbing now, truly terrified.

The wind and rain were whipping the house. But the burning pain in Tia's chest obliterated everything.

"Call 911," Leander barked at Heddy.

Only dimly, as if he were shouting from a long way away did Tia hear him.

"Am I dying?" Tia managed in a shaken voice.

Leander turned back to her, his eyes very kind, his gentle tone reassuring. "It's going to be all right. There's nothing to be afraid of."

But he was wrong.

Tia buried her head in his shoulder and wept. They were tears of despair and agony. But there was something else— fear. The most terrible fear she had ever known.

Fear of what she had done.

Never before had she been afraid to die. And it was all Leander's fault.

Pictures from the past flashed before her. She was remembering the sanitarium, the patients roaming the wide halls, their vacant stares, the wild horror of her husband's illness and his rampages. She saw scraps of paper blackening in the library trash basket, and then the thick noxious smoke filling the library. Next she saw Barret's decaying body in the ravine and the Beretta lying in the sand by his skeletal claw.

For years she had never once allowed herself to think of these things. But now she was too weak to suppress the terrifying memories.

A crushing wave of pain spiked from her chest down her left arm.

Heddy knelt and kneaded her age-spotted hand. "The ambulance is coming—"

"Too late," Tia gasped. And then she looked straight at Leander and spewed all the jealous venom in her heart. "This is your fault. First you took Heddy. Then you murdered Barret. Now, you have killed me. Why couldn't you just stay away?"

Tears sprang to Heddy's eyes.

Leander's gaze hardened, but he didn't speak.

Tia was suddenly too exhausted to say more. She saw the blackened ashes at the bottom of the library trash can. She remembered opening the windows to get rid of the smell of smoke.

And then she felt herself slipping into darkness.

"If I die, promise me, Heddy darling, that you won't take him back."

Only dimly was she aware of Heddy's face crumpling as she made a sharp little cry.

"Promise me."

Heddy was very pale as she leaned down and whispered brokenly. Tia smiled faintly at her granddaughter's words.

She had won. Now—at last, she, Tia, could rest. She wanted peace. Oblivion.

But when she closed her eyes that was not what she found.

One minute she was drifting into darkness with the memories of her long life passing before her.

In the next she was being sucked into a vacuum of fire and sent hurtling into a blazing hell.

Waves of flame writhed like snakes around her.

Terrified, she screamed.

The snakes slithered closer, wrapping themselves around her ankles, pulling her deeper into the inferno.

She heard Leander's kind voice through the spiraling orange tongues that coiled ever tighter.

But she couldn't see him. She couldn't find him.

And she had to.

She opened her eyes, but he wasn't there, either.

She was lost in a sea of fiery darkness.

"Leander—"

"Don't try to talk," he said soothingly.

But she had to talk. She had to tell him.

Before it was too late.

But just as she was about to explain, the sky seemed to crash down upon her, and she was trapped in a fiery pyre with the burning writhing snakes.

Seven

There was a roar from the angry crowd when Leander emerged from the hospital into the grayness of the day.

"Knight!"

Leander didn't hear them at first as he raced down the steps. The rain had stopped. The gray clouds were higher, and the sun had broken through.

The Santa Claus and his sleigh that was set up in front of the hospital looked oddly out of place on the lush green lawn. The day was almost balmy—at least to someone used to the bitter winter of southern Alaska.

Not that Leander even noticed the weather. Or the Christmas decorations.

His skin was sallow, and there were dark smudges of sleeplessness under his eyes.

"Knight! Murderer!"

Leander's mouth went dry when he heard his name; it

grew absolutely parched when he saw the stampeding army hurrying angrily up the steps toward him.

Townspeople with raised fists were waving handmade signs. Yates and his deputies in their uniforms trying to hold back the crowd.

Photographers screamed abuse and curses, so Leander would scowl their way.

Two smiling reporters rushed through the melee with raised mikes. One of them was a tall, slim woman with curly black hair. She had a nice smile and nice eyes. A rhinestone snowflake was pinned to her lapel. In other circumstances he might have liked her as a friend.

"Bastard! You belong in a cell!"

Leander ducked the mikes and cameras.

"Murderer!"

Venomous insults erupted like lava as he bolted for the rear parking lot where Jim Bob's cousin had sworn he'd left the truck.

"Get the bastard!"

More shouts. Thundering heels on pavement. Storm troopers right behind him. In hot pursuit.

They were catching him.

"You deserve the same thing Tia got!"

They closed in around him when he reached Jim Bob's truck.

"Murderer!"

One of the photographers cursed him vilely.

Leander's lips curled back from his teeth. He grabbed one of the signs and, raising it, turned on the photographer. His black eyes lit dangerously. He made an inarticulate animal sound of rage and drew back the sign as if he might strike.

The photographer laughed gleefully. Flashes blazed. Cameras clicked.

"Got the bastard!"

More creepy photographs for the tabloids.

"Why did you come back to Kinney?" the nice reporter asked.

"Because that's what my kid wanted for Christmas. Because I thought I was still in love with my wife."

"Did you kill—"

"Go to hell. All of you."

Leander threw down his sign and got in his truck, slamming the door as the pretty young woman scribbled and the photographers got shots of the sign he'd thrown down.

He fumbled on the floorboard for the keys. His heart was pounding at a terrific rate and with such terrific force that his whole body shook. He couldn't believe he'd answered the woman's question.

His tormentors got on either side of his truck and began rocking it back and forth. Suddenly he felt exactly like one of his heroes in a novel, hemmed in by enemies.

Trapped. Claustrophobic.

At the sound of breaking glass he jumped. He felt a small sharp pain in his left cheek. Touching the place with a fingertip, he drew back a splinter of glass and blood.

The bastards had smashed out a back window. A flying shard had cut his face.

Somehow he managed to start the truck and back out of the parking lot without running over one of the jerks.

Once he'd escaped them, Leander drove slowly. The road was straight; the south Texas landscape bleak and endless. The sky was huge.

He mopped his brow. He could feel his pulse pounding under the bandage over his temple. His blood pressure was probably off the charts.

For eight years Heddy had put him in hell. After the way she'd treated him last night, he was finally through.

Tia had hovered in intensive care on the brink of death all night, her condition too unstable for surgery. Leander had stayed in the hospital to be with Heddy. Not that she had wanted him there.

Heddy had neither looked at him, nor spoken to him. Every time he'd tried to comfort her, she'd pushed him away with a wild desperate look and curled up in a vinyl chair, hugging herself quietly or silently weeping.

Her tears would have been bad enough, but what killed him was the way she'd kept staring at him with her soulful blue eyes and repeating, "I should never have chased after you. I should have stayed with Marcus last night. If I had, Tia would be all right."

She wanted Marcus! That pale, bloodless, aristocratic wimp!

Finally she said that one time too many. Or maybe he'd just had one cup of coffee too many.

Whatever. He'd flung his coffee cup in the trash and erupted.

"Fine," he'd yelled. "Go back to Marcus. I'm sick of the way you let Tia run your life. Not matter what I do, I can never come up to your high standards or hers. You want Marcus? You want a divorce? Okay—you've got it."

When she'd chased after him, he'd shrugged her off and sworn to her that this time he was really through.

Half an hour later when he got to his cabin and his phone was ringing, he was so worried about her, fool that he was, he raced inside and grabbed it.

A brutal masculine voice that sounded a whole lot like Benson's blasted him. "Bastard! Get out of town. Next time we won't miss."

Leander turned on his television and Yates was there, expounding pompously from the hospital steps. Leander punched the remote and was stunned to find Mary Ann giving an idiotic critique of his novel *Dead Ringer*.

Then Heddy walked into the shop, and the reporters pounced on her.

"Tell our viewers about your famous husband."

Heddy's eyes were swimming with tears as she looked directly into the camera. "Would you please just leave us alone?"

On another channel he saw his own haggard image swinging a sign that read Murderer, Go Back to Alaska. He listened to the pretty reporter ask him why he'd come back to Kinney. He heard himself say, "Because I thought I still loved my wife."

Leander caught his breath. He couldn't stand it.

His agent called next.

Partly to express concern.

Mostly to inform him that his publisher was putting a rush on a huge reprint order to get more books out to meet the demand.

"They're selling like hotcakes!"

Leander went ballistic. "You just don't get it, Shaw. Nobody does! I'm not some psycho killer. I didn't come here to get shot at or to terrorize an old lady into a heart attack just to sell a few lousy books. I came here to try to save my marriage and get to know my daughter."

"Sure. Sure. I'm on your side. But, hey, nobody up here is complaining if we sell a few million more copies of your novels just because a few idiots believe—"

Leander swore viciously and slammed the phone down.

He was losing it. And there wasn't a damn thing he could do about it.

When the telephone rang again, he picked it up, intending to force out some sort of apology to Dean.

"Shaw, look, I'm—"

A deep voice cut in, "Leave Heddy alone! Go back to Alaska, killer!"

This time Leander didn't bother to hang up.

Heddy wasn't going to call. She didn't believe in him. She never would. She didn't give a damn what he might be going through.

Hell. He had said he was going to divorce her.

It was about time he got smart and stuck to what any fool could see was the only rational solution to their crazy marriage.

Maybe he still loved her. Maybe she still felt something for him.

So what? He couldn't live on *maybe*.

She was worse than the jerks who had mobbed him at the hospital. Her only concern was Tia, and Tia ruled her the same way she ruled the town. If Tia died, Heddy would blame him for her death, too.

Leander sank onto his bed and stared up at the crooked chandelier. The caller had it right. The only smart thing to do was to get the hell back to Alaska.

Who would miss him?

He thought of Christina. Of Heddy.

He was only making their lives worse by hanging around. He was mortally sick of the whole mess.

Not that he could go before Tia's crisis was resolved.

Still, he got up and began listlessly stacking his things in a pile, so they would be easy to pack when the time came.

As he grabbed an armful of hangers from his closet, he heard tires crunching into his shell drive. Tensing, he backed warily away from his window. But the footsteps running lightly up his steps and across his porch were a woman's, and the knock at the door was gentle enough to be Heddy's.

He felt a sudden tearing pain. His whole being ached for her to walk through that door and tell him that she loved him and believed in him.

Cautiously he went to the door and opened it. But his smile died when he saw the beautiful woman standing there.

In the slanting afternoon sun, Mary Ann's lush hair looked like flyaway plumes of fire. Her beige sweater was too tight across her beautiful breasts. She was as brightly painted and as ravishingly aglow as a stage actress. There was a sexy interplay between her mouth and eyes that probably caught most men.

He froze, unable to think of a thing to say to her.

With a bat of her long lashes, she cued him boldly. "I'm sure you don't mind if I come in."

"Anytime." He held the door for her.

"Hey," she said softly, touching his nicked cheek and bandaged temple. "This town isn't so good for your health."

"I'm not the town's most popular citizen."

"With me you are."

She squeezed past him then, letting her lush body brush his.

"Sorry," she whispered.

But she wasn't, and her warm smile made him uneasy.

"You're here because . . ."

"Oh, er, yes. I—I brought my book."

He relaxed just a little when he saw the fat brown package she was carrying.

"You do remember you promised to read it?"

He didn't, but he nodded anyway.

"I just think it's terrible what everybody's saying about you. I don't believe you'd hurt a fly. Much less blow out your father-in-law's brains and leave him for the buzzards to eat."

Leander's mouth tightened. "You said you came because of your book?"

"I know it's probably a terrible time for you, but I want you to tell me every little thing that's wrong with it," she purred. "I can take criticism."

"Sure. I'll get to it when I can."

"I—I thought maybe we could read it . . . together?" Her voice was throaty.

"Like you said—it's a bad time."

"Oh." Her painted lips pouted prettily.

He didn't reverse his position.

"I tried to call, but your line was busy."

"Write down your phone number and address. I'll get back to you when I'm done," he said in a businesslike tone.

She wrote quickly. "I'll be waiting . . . breathlessly for your call."

"It may be a while," he warned dryly.

Her teasing eyes were too intimate as he escorted her outside. Just as he was putting her into her car, Heddy drove up.

She looked pale and exhausted as she cut her engine. But Leander's throat went hot at the sight of her.

Heddy had come to him. Why?

He would have rushed to her if he hadn't played the fool for her so many times before. With an effort, he forced himself to pretend indifference and concentrate on his first guest. He kept talking to Mary Ann even though his real attention was riveted to the solitary woman in the Suburban.

His flirty grin produced a dazzling smile from Mary Ann. Heddy whitened and pulled down her visor and fluffed her fingers through her hair.

When Mary Ann made him an illicit proposition, Leander leaned deeper into her car, kissed her cheek and whispered his regrets that he was a married man. As he did it, he relished the way Heddy slammed the visor back in place, the way her face tightened.

Was she jealous? Did she feel something for him after all?

He beamed brightly and waved at Mary Ann as she drove away. Only when she was out of sight did he lower his hand and walk slowly over to Heddy's Suburban.

"You getting out? Or are you just going to sit there fiddling with your hair all afternoon?"

"You didn't look like you would welcome an interruption," she retorted icily.

"Didn't I? Sorry."

"Mary Ann told me she was going to the bank."

"I assure you, her visit was strictly professional," he said mildly.

"I'll bet."

"Would you care if it wasn't? I mean, since you're so determined to blame me for everything that goes wrong—"

She didn't answer as he helped her down from the Suburban. Instead she looked at the bare branches of the large oak tree to the right of his front door. One of the branches had broken in the storm and had collapsed against his roof. Dead brown leaves, soaked by the rain, littered his porch and shell drive.

"Either you or Jim Bob needs to do some serious pruning—"

"It'll have to be Jim Bob. He's hell with a chain saw."

Leander was leading her inside his cabin. "Besides, as you can see—" Once inside, Leander turned his broad back to her and made a careless gesture toward the messy pile of jackets and jeans and luggage by his computer and manuscripts. "I'm leaving just as soon as we know what's going to happen to Tia."

He heard Heddy sink to the bed. "Oh. I—I..." Her distressed voice sounded almost faint.

Still, he kept his back to her and continued to pretend indifference. He was divorcing her. He was through with her *forever* he reminded himself. It didn't matter that she had come to see him.

"Leander, I came here because—I know I made you feel terrible. I want to thank you for being so sweet to Tia last night and to me when we were both so awful to you. Whenever I'm around her, it's like I—"

"You can only be loyal to her by hating me," he said, finishing her sentence and turning to face her at last.

"That's what Mary Ann said to me this morning. I guess, in a way, you're right. But, I don't know what I would have done without you. You were wonderful in the ambulance. I totally panicked— And when you blew up and left the hospital a while ago, I panicked again. I—I don't think I can go through this without you."

Leander stared at her in amazement. "Even if it means more scandal and publicity, and making Tia unhappy?"

"I can see that the publicity is worse for you than it is for me."

That admission, as well as her gratitude, further stunned him.

"And Tia?"

Guiltily she looked away.

He gritted his teeth. *He was through, damn it.*

"Most of all, you need to stay for Christina's sake," Heddy continued on a different tack. "I just left her. I'm afraid she's seen the television coverage, and she's very upset and confused. Until Tia's better, I'm going to have to be at the hospital a lot, and Christina needs somebody to stay with her. I think it should be you."

He nodded wearily. She wanted him to stay more for Christina than for her.

"There's something else. Tia has been asking for you. When we try to distract her, she gets very agitated and starts repeating your name over and over. Sort of like a chant."

Leander stared at her angrily. With her dying breath, that domineering old witch still wanted his hide. "Wait till the press hears this," he muttered, furious. "It's not enough that she nailed me to the cross for Barret's death. She's not about to die until she makes damn sure she's convinced everybody—including you—that I brought on this heart attack. Or maybe she's going to say I poisoned her."

"Leander, she really is so pitiful."

"Yeah, sure." His low voice was harsh.

"I—I don't blame you for feeling—"

Confusion, grief, pain—he saw them all in her luminous eyes. If he was going to divorce her, it would be easier if he hated her.

His fury left him.

Slowly he crossed the room and sat down on the bed beside her, enfolding her in his arms. She laid her golden head upon his shoulder.

"Forgive me. I shouldn't have said that. You know I hope Tia gets better."

"I'm so afraid she won't," Heddy whispered in a small voice. "I feel like I'm losing everything."

"I can relate to that."

With an effort he put Tia out of his mind and concentrated on Heddy. She was shivering as she huddled against him. He drew her deeper into his arms, warming her, soothing her. Then he buried his face in the wealth of her hair and murmured reassurances that everything would be all right, even as his own doubts tore at him.

She moaned softly and clung to him.

"Lie down with me," he prodded gently a little while later.

"No. I—" She shivered and tried to pull away.

"Heddy," he whispered softly. "I just want to hold you for a little while. I swear I won't touch you in any other way."

She sucked in a hesitant breath. "I don't know—"

"One last time."

She looked into his eyes.

As always, even though she looked pale and exhausted, he found her beautiful. As always, in her gaze he saw her soul.

God, he'd had her last night. Since then she'd put him through hell. He was going to divorce her. But even as he longed to despise her, he was starving for her.

"I won't touch you," he said, swallowing hard.

She bit her lip. "That's okay," she whispered, her voice as low and choked as his.

Very slowly her arms went around his neck, and she allowed him to ease her down on the bed beside him.

As she stretched her cool, pliant body against his warm length, he was sure he'd never known such exquisite torture. He closed his eyes to shut out the vision of her lush beauty; he clenched his fists so he would not run them over her body. He was determined not to let his desire for her break the tenderness of this short time they had together.

She snuggled closer against him, sighing, as if she felt warm and safe in his arms. Gently he brushed his lips against her hair, then her brow.

He had wanted a life with her so desperately. It broke his heart that he might never hold her like this again, that he would probably never make love to her again. But he couldn't go on like this.

It would tear him apart to leave her, but as he pressed her closer, he knew he was at the end of his rope. He was through fighting a losing battle.

Baby-sitting had to be the most stressful job in the world, Leander thought, eyeing his wristwatch as he had dozens of times before, glad that it was about time for Heddy to return.

"Can I wear your hat, Uncle Leander?" Attilla asked very politely—which would have warned Leander that the brat had something up his sleeve. "I want to see the bullet hole in it again."

Attilla was hanging his last Christmas ornament on the almost leafless, stunted mesquite tree that Leander and the children had chopped down. They had hauled it up three flights of stairs to their playroom, leaving a trail of mesquite twigs and thorns that had kept two housekeepers busy with brooms and sweepers for an hour.

Christina pranced saucily over to the window in her daddy's Stetson. "No! You had your turn, Attilla!" She shivered involuntarily in spite of the thick blue sweater she was wearing.

Cleo who was standing by the tree, threw down the little cowboy hat that she'd been making for a miniature Santa and dashed up to Christina on swift bare feet. "I haven't had my turn yet!"

"That's because my daddy's hat is way too big for you, Cleo." At just that moment, the Stetson tumbled over Christina's brow and hid her eyes.

"See there. It doesn't fit you, either," Cleo said importantly.

Christina pushed the black brim back up. "Does, too!"

"Children, I may just have to wear my hat myself—if you all can't share."

The quick treble of worried voices rose in volume as each child pleaded his case to Leander. All afternoon they had besieged him with questions. And with demands that he settle countless circular arguments. Attilla and Christina had almost come to blows about which baby mesquite tree would make the perfect "Cowboy Christmas" tree. Then Cleo had to be comforted and bandaged with three Band-Aid strips after she got a mesquite thorn wedged under her thumbnail.

Never had Leander felt more powerful. Nor more important.

Nor more stressed out. Maybe because he was used to so much solitude. Maybe because he wasn't used to so much energy.

This fatherhood bit could be nerve shredding. Each child had a totally different personality. Attilla was a hyperactive dynamo who turned into a bully if he didn't get constant attention. Christina was bossy, selfish and passionately stubborn. Cleo tended to whine about the smallest injury, imagined or real, and she couldn't keep up with her shoes to save her soul.

All three were daredevils. All three were argumentative. All three were full of ideas. But their way of viewing the most ordinary things in life with a marvelous, wide-eyed wonder sparked his creativity.

Leander had thought he was messy, but these kids were as hard on a neat house as three miniature cyclones. Nevertheless, the pluses of fatherhood outweighed the minuses. At least that's what he thought until Attilla yanked the Stetson off Christina's head, jammed it on top of his own red corkscrews, raced out onto the landing, jumped onto the banister and slid recklessly all the way down to the foyer, screaming, "Yahoo, ride 'em cowboy!" at the top of his lungs. His oversize athletic shoes hit the black and white marble floor running.

Leander was about to race after him. But Christina's question stopped him cold.

"Did you really kill my grandpa?"

Leander heard the front door bang which meant Attilla had escaped. Christina watched him, her blue eyes charged with passionate curiosity.

"Who told you that, sweetheart?" he demanded mildly. "Your mother?"

"No. Kids. People in town. Mr. Yates on TV. I saw you, too, and you looked mean."

Leander sank to his knees and ruffled her hair. "It isn't true, and someday everybody will know it isn't."

"A kid at school told a lie about me once."

Leander nodded sympathetically.

"And everybody believed him instead of me." A pause. "Does my mommy believe you?"

"No. And I'm afraid that when she does learn the truth, it'll probably be too late for us."

Christina chewed her lip. Big-eyed, Cleo was listening to them and studying her bandaged thumb.

"I believe you, Daddy," Christina said at last.

Christina climbed onto his knee and put her arms around his neck.

"I believe you, too, Uncle Leander," Cleo said in a hushed voice. When she came up to him cautiously, he pulled her into his arms too.

"And, girls, that means a whole lot to me," he said, his voice oddly muffled. "More than you'll ever know."

Christina who could not stay serious long wriggled to the carpet. "You're the best baby-sitter we ever had. Are you going to whip Attilla when we find him?"

Cleo said, "It was my turn to wear your hat. And he made me hurt my thumb."

Leander had the distinct feeling he was being manipulated by minds that were far more clever than his. But there was no way he could disappoint his only two allies.

"Let's go get him!" he whispered.

The girls were out on the landing in a flash. And before Leander could groan "Not the banister" they had straddled it and were flying down the three flights even faster than Attilla had.

What the hell? If three brats could do it—

Leander climbed on the polished railing and sailed after them.

He came flying into the marble-floored foyer just as Heddy, her arms full of packages, burst through the front door.

"Leander! What do you think you're doing?"

"Er... baby-sitting."

The little girls giggled madly from the corner where they were turning a crystal ball upside down and then setting it upright, so they could watch tiny flecks of fake snow shower down on the brightly painted Santa Claus inside.

"Mommy—" Christina was shaking the ball vigorously. "Daddy's going to catch Attilla for us and spank him."

"I thought I told you that we don't allow corporal punishment in this house," Heddy said primly.

Leander sprang from the banister. "I wasn't going to spank him. I just wanted to find him."

"And the banister?"

He grinned sheepishly, charmingly. "I couldn't let the girls escape, too."

Heddy relented and gave him a soft smile. "You're as incorrigible as Attilla." A pause. "So, how did it go today?"

"A piece of cake," he lied.

She smiled. "Hey, you're getting pretty good at this."

"Kids take some getting used to when you've lived alone like I have for so long. But I think baby-sitting might grow on me."

For an instant her glowing face looked delicate and vulnerable, and he allowed himself to dream that they could be a real family. That she could really be his wife again. That he could take care of her and the children.

Leander swallowed, fighting the constriction in his throat. A frown chased away her own smile.

"How's Tia?" he asked, growing serious, too.

"Better."

"Then?"

"We have to talk," she said, her voice faltering.

"Okay."

The afternoon sun was streaming across the verandah as Heddy led Leander outside. But the horizon was dotted with dark clouds.

"So why do you look so worried if Tia's better?"

"She's conscious," Heddy said evasively.

He pressed her hand. "I'm glad."

Heddy tugged her hand free of his. "Conscious. But . . . restless. Not quite herself. She won't talk to anybody but you. She keeps talking about hell and damnation and the devil . . . and—"

"And?"

"And then you. All in the same breath."

"That figures," he said bitterly.

"She says she won't say a word unless Tom Yates and the press are there, too. She wants them to hear what she says to you. Because she might only have the strength to say it once."

Leander sucked in his breath. It had to be a real bombshell then. Dear God. What was left for her to do that could possibly make things worse between himself and Heddy? After all, they were getting a divorce.

"Do you have any idea what she's going to say?" he asked dully.

Heddy shook her head, but he could tell by her pale face that she was just as worried as he was.

The old witch probably had a vial of arsenic or something tucked away in a bedroom drawer somewhere with his fingerprints all over it. She'd probably say he held her down and forced her to drink it.

With an effort he suppressed his novelist's imagination. "Let's go then," he whispered. "We might as well get it over with."

Eight

The crowded hospital room, which smelled faintly of antiseptic, had gay pink wallpaper and was cheerily lit.

Heddy's heart was full of dread as she stepped inside.

"Tia, look who's here," Heddy said in a soft tone as she led a grim Leander past Tom Yates, Marcus, and a pretty journalist with curly dark hair to the thin figure in the bed.

Tia's skin was the color and texture of parchment, and her thin strands of gray hair were glued to her skull. Her droopy eyelids and the blue rings under her eyes made her look wan and exhausted, even though she was wide awake.

In contrast, Leander, who was huge and dark and muscular, exuded robust health and strapping energy as he loomed over the elderly woman.

What could Tia be thinking of to demand to see him when she was so ill? When their mutual dislike was so evident.

Tia's rheumy, sunken eyes regarded him warily. Leander's jaw muscles trembled despite his efforts to set his teeth.

When he pulled up a chair to sit down beside her, Tia recoiled weakly, an exertion which brought on desperate choking sounds.

"Tia! Nurse!" Heddy cried, pushing Leander aside and attempting to soothe her grandmother. "There's nothing to be afraid of, Tia. I'm right here. Leander's not going to hurt you."

Lights danced frantically across her four monitors. An alarm went off. White-coated nurses came running in to adjust tubes and dials.

"I'm sorry, folks," the R.N. said, regarding them all, especially Leander, with immense suspicion. "We have too many visitors." Her tone sharpened. "You, Mr. Knight, definitely have to go."

Leander's dark face hardened. But when he started to rise, Tia's gnarled hand seized the nurse's skirt and sent tongue depressors flying out of her coat pocket.

"Make him stay. I *have* to talk to him in front of all these people. And I don't care if it kills me."

"There! There!" Heddy whispered pleadingly. "There's no need to be so melodramatic, Tia."

Tia clawed at her, too.

Heddy took her palsied hand. "We can do this tomorrow just as well as today."

"No...no..." Tia's faint grip tightened. She began mumbling, rapidly, hoarsely. Most of what she said was gibberish. What came through was her fear and her fierce determination to speak to Leander.

"I hate you, Pepper Knight. I do hate you," Tia whispered, her voice so low it was almost inaudible. "But I'm going to hell if I don't tell these people the truth about you."

A muscle in Leander's jaw ticked violently under his dark skin as he leaned closer to his old adversary.

"She's delirious," the bossy nurse said tartly. "Mr. Knight, you need to go."

"No—" Tia rasped. "I do hate him."

"With good reason," Yates encouraged.

"Let her talk," Leander said forcefully. "Can't you see she isn't strong enough to argue with all of you?"

Tia looked into Heddy's eyes pleadingly. "I've done your husband a . . . a terrible wrong."

"How, Tia?" Heddy prompted gently.

"He . . . Pepper didn't kill your father."

The room went deathly quiet as everyone waited in breathless suspense for Tia to continue. Yates stepped closer to the bed.

She took her time; sometimes her words were slurred and halting. Sometimes her tired voice was so low she had to repeat whole sentences. But her listeners hung on her every tortured word.

"I—I knew Pepper was innocent, but I kept silent. Not because I wanted to protect him and the Kinney name. But because I wanted them, especially you, Heddy, to *think* he was guilty and that I was covering up for him because he was your husband. Because I wanted to protect the Kinney name."

Leander's color had heightened.

So had Heddy's. "Tia, no. You couldn't have deliberately—"

"I—I did. I loved you, girl. A fool could see Pepper wasn't half good enough for you. I wanted the best for you. Not some . . . some poor nobody with no family like him."

"What are you saying?"

"Barret shot himself!"

The floor seemed to rock beneath Heddy's feet, and Heddy had to lean heavily against the bed to steady herself. "I don't believe it!"

"I knew he killed himself." Tia's pitiful voice cracked. "And I knew why. I knew everything. But I kept it to myself."

"Oh, Tia—"

"You see, I found Barret's suicide note after that awful fight in the library. You had taken Leander upstairs. I discovered Leander's gun was missing, too. Barret said in his note he'd taken it and was going to kill himself in that ravine so he wouldn't make a mess near the house, and so Heddy and I wouldn't have to find him like that."

Leander was innocent!

And all these years she hadn't allowed herself to believe him! All these years she'd felt sorry for Tia and had tried to be the perfect granddaughter to make up for bringing Leander into their lives.

Heddy's heart screamed in silent joy and agony. She had hurt Leander terribly. She had driven him away. Why? Why had she so blindly believed Tia? Why had she listened to all the mean things the small-minded gossips had been so eager to say against him?

He hadn't cared about what any of them had thought. Only her. And she had let him down in the most terrible way a wife could let her husband down. She had banished him to that lonely hell in Alaska. She had kept Christina from him. Her crime against him was a thousand times worse than Tia's.

When Heddy put a soft, apologetic hand on Leander's wide shoulder, he stiffened as if her touch were now repugnant to him.

"I want to hear it all," he said, his swarthy face grimly fierce, his dark eyes cool and emotionless as he regarded her. "Let her finish."

Heddy's hand fell limply to her side.

Tia went on with her confessional. "I knew what Barret intended to do, and I didn't try to stop him. I didn't send anybody after him. If anybody murdered my son, it was me. In his note he begged Pepper to forgive him."

"Why, Tia? Why would Daddy, who had everything—"

Tia's guilty voice was muffled. "Barret had gone to see a doctor in San Antonio and found out what we both suspected, that he had a rapidly growing tumor in his brain. He knew just how terrible it would be because his own father had died the same way."

The blood drained from Heddy's face. "I—I should have known. He'd been acting so strangely. He lost his temper at the least little thing."

"How could you have known? We never told you the truth about your grandfather. We took Gerald to a hospital in New Orleans. Gerald was so violent at the end—completely out of his mind. He hated me, Barret, everybody. Barret said he could feel the sickness in his brain getting worse. In his note he said that every day he felt a little crazier, a little more prone to irrational rages. He knew from what had happened to his father what would happen to him. He said in his note that if you hadn't come into the library when you did, he would have kept hitting Leander with that lamp till he killed him. His last words were, 'Forgive me for this act of selfish cowardice, but remember that if I were a horse, you'd put me out of my misery.'"

"Oh, Tia, why didn't you show us the note?"

"Because I saw my chance to get rid of that cocky upstart you'd so foolishly married, once and for all. I burned it in the library fireplace. I thought I was doing the smart thing. I thought it would be best for everybody—especially you."

Leander got up. Towering over everybody in the room, his frozen face was a dark unreadable mask. Heddy felt a shaft of real fear as he avoided touching her or looking at her.

"Well, now you know, don't you, Sugar?" His mouth was a thin cruel line; his wide-shouldered body rigid.

"Leander, I'm—"

"Don't start! Not now when it's too late."

Her blood ran cold at the grimness in his tone. "Leander, please. You have to forgive me. This changes—"

But he was already gone.

Heddy was about to run after him, but Marcus grabbed her arm gently. His brotherly voice was kind and mild. "Let him go. He needs time alone."

"I—I thought it would be for the best." Tia's thin voice trailed off miserably as Marcus led Heddy back to the bed.

"But it wasn't, Tia," Heddy whispered.

"When you were in labor with Christina, you sobbed so brokenheartedly for Pepper. You wanted him back so much, I thought I would go mad. But when Pepper came to the hospital and begged to see you, I told him you didn't want to see him."

When Heddy gave a cry of loss and desolation, Marcus circled her with his arms. And because his embrace held friendship and nothing more, she welcomed it.

"Forgive me?" Tia whined in a strangled whisper, fretfully clutching for Heddy's hand. *"Please."*

Suddenly Heddy's eyes were swimming as she thought of the terrible burden her grandmother had carried all these years.

"Oh, Tia. My guilt is so much worse than yours."

The pretty journalist rushed out with her story.

Nobody saw Leander when he returned to the door a minute or two later. Nobody saw him stop dead still in the doorway, his black eyes fierce, not a muscle flickering in his face when he saw Heddy wrapped in Marcus's arms.

Nobody saw him leave without saying a word.

A cool sea mist was rolling in from the bay when Heddy drove past the reporters and television crews, who were besieging the guards she had posted at her ranch gates. The fog was swirling thicker when she reached Leander's cabin and parked her Suburban.

For two days she had waited in an agony of suspense for Leander to call her at the hospital or to come by the ranch. Since her confession Tia had improved rapidly. It was Heddy who felt sick and tired and more afraid than she had ever felt in her life.

She was being vilified in the press as the rich wife who hadn't stood by her husband. But it wasn't the unflattering publicity that was killing her, it was Leander's cold withdrawal.

Marcus had advised her to wait, to give Leander more time.

But she simply had to try to see him. If necessary she would gladly go down on her knees and beg his forgiveness. She had to tell him how desperately sorry she was.

If only he would listen. If only he would believe her.

For more than eight long years she had refused to believe him. And now he said he wanted a divorce.

Heddy quietly went up to his door and laid her hand upon the rough wood. She was about to knock, but when she touched it, it swung open a little.

She heard a woman's voice and then Leander's husky laughter.

She couldn't see them, but she knew they had to be sitting on the small red couch by his fireplace. Mary Ann's voice was low and vibrant. She was speaking with such intensity that Heddy caught every syllable.

"You've been so wonderful, Pepper."

"My pleasure, M.A."

They were using pet names for each other.

"You're so experienced. So talented. How can I ever repay you?"

"Easily," he murmured. "So easily."

The intimacy and warmth in his husky voice wounded Heddy greatly. She imagined any of a dozen ways a woman as beautiful and flirtatious as Mary Ann could please a man of Leander's virile appetites.

In the silence that followed, Heddy envisioned them embracing, kissing. And much more.

A log crackled in the fireplace.

A plume of gray smoke erupted from the chimney and swirled upward in the fog.

Heddy shrank away from the door, feeling lost and hopeless.

Then without uttering a sound to let them know she had ever been there, she fled hurriedly down the steps into the mist.

The central heater in the big house was broken, and Heddy and her two little girls and Mayflower, Christina's golden dog, were huddled in blankets on the carpet around a Chinese checkerboard in the playroom.

"Mommy, do you think the poor children will like all their presents?" Christina demanded with shining eyes.

Heddy looked up from their checkerboard to the messy pile of gifts that were under, or rather stacked around, the leafless "Cowboy Christmas" tree.

"They'll love them, darling."

"They'd better, even if my bows aren't good, 'cause my thumb hurts," Cleo complained, sneaking her marble an extra space since they weren't looking. "It hurts something awful from wrapping so many. And I'm cold." She opened her mouth so Heddy could see how dramatically she could make her teeth chatter.

"This year there's more than a hundred gifts," Heddy said, pulling a second blanket snugly over Cleo.

"A hundred and seven," Cleo stated proudly.

Heddy and the girls knew this because Attilla had counted the gifts five times. He was a slow, meticulous counter. He'd spent more time racing about, hollering numbers out, than wrapping. Which had brought complaints from the more dutiful girls.

"When is the fat church lady coming by for them?"

"Girls, if dear Mrs. Gumphrey heard you call her fat, she would be so hurt."

One minute Heddy was laughing and telling the girls they needed to carry all the gifts down to the foyer. In the next she heard a man's heavy boots on the stairs and Christina's joyous scream nearly piercing her eardrum.

"Daddy!"

"Uncle Pepper!"

The checkerboard went flying, and so did the marbles. Mayflower galloped after her miniature mistresses and jumped up on Leander, too, big friendly paws leaving gray smudges on his white shirtfront.

Heddy got up from the floor slowly, miserably, and then just stood there, curling her bare toes into the carpet as she watched Leander bend his tall body down to pet the dog and embrace his daughter and Cleo—and deliberately ignore his wife.

Heddy was barefoot, in old jeans and an old yellow sweater, with masses of gleaming tangles flowing over her shoulders like molten gold. If only she'd known he was coming today, she would have combed her hair or put on makeup. Then he couldn't have resisted looking at her. As it was, she was as pale as a rabbit. The cold was penetrating the soles of her feet and her thin jeans and causing her to shiver.

When he raised his black head from the children, his eyes locked with Heddy's for a long moment. She willed one kind word, one tiny sign that he still cared as their gazes held.

But his dark face was shuttered and colder even than the chill of the unheated house.

"Oh, hello," was all he said—casually in that tight, controlled tone she hated.

Her blue eyes narrowed. Suddenly she was remembering that Jim Yates had told her that Leander had driven Mary Ann into Corpus Christi for a late dinner the night before, that they hadn't come back till dawn.

Everywhere she had gone that morning to do her last-minute Christmas shopping, everyone had sneaked side-long, curious glances at her, and every busybody had seen fit to repeat that story or add to it.

"I saw Jim Bob's truck parked under the water tower last night till all hours. Looked to me like there was a man and a woman inside."

"Couldn't see much of 'em though."

That was something Heddy hated about Kinney. If ever a person took a false step or a husband did something a wife wouldn't like, there was no keeping discreetly silent about it.

"You're shivering," Leander said awkwardly to Heddy.

"The heater's broken. A repairman's coming." Heddy's voice was as strained as his as she picked up a blanket and draped it around her shoulders.

"Daddy, can I wear your hat?" Christina asked Leander.

He smiled and handed it to her.

Peeping out from under the wide black brim of his Stetson, Christina asked him, "Why haven't you been by like you promised?"

The two adults stared at each other in mute dismay.

Only when Leander realized he was looking at Heddy, did he pull his eyes away and answer his daughter.

"Well, sweetheart, I'm here now," Leander said lightly, offering no other explanation.

"Are...are you in love with Mary Ann? Have you been visiting her instead? Are you going to divorce my mommy?" Christina asked. "Everybody in town and on TV says that Mommy was mean not to believe you—"

Heddy's fingers tightened on the soft woolen blanket. *Oh, how fast the gossips forgot their own fault. Oh, how much more fun to make her the new villain.*

People had always talked about her and all the Kinneys. But it was different now with the truth out about Leander's innocence. He had the town's sympathy, indeed the whole country's, while she, the wife who had not stood by him—

"Everybody in town should keep their damn mouths shut," Leander began impatiently, taking Heddy's side, before he caught himself.

"Christina," Heddy protested. "You shouldn't listen to idle gossip."

"How the hell can she help it in this town?" Leander demanded. "When everywhere you go—"

"You know what else they say, Mommy? They say you're going to divorce Daddy and marry Marcus 'cause Tia wants you to," Christina persisted.

"Maybe the gossips have it figured for once," Leander said grimly.

"No," Christina said. Her voice was a murmur, but her blue eyes were fierce as she looked from him to her mother. "'Cause if you divorce him, I'll run away!" Drama and passion were carrying her away. "I'll run all the way to Alaska! Even if I freeze...and die. Even if...even if I miss Christmas and don't get a single present."

"Can I come, too?" Cleo begged in a small lost voice. When she paused to catch her breath, her teeth began to chatter. "But can I bring...just one little-bitty Christmas present?"

Nine

Leander gave little heed to where he was going as he strode down the circular drive past the palms to his truck. He was intent on only one thing—getting away from Heddy. She had been laughing and playing happily with the girls before he'd come in. Then her smiles had died.

All it had taken to convince him once and for all to head back to Alaska was the way her lovely face had been pale with misery every time she'd looked at him. Her obvious agony at his presence had been almost worse to endure than the contempt she'd felt for him when she'd believed he was a killer.

"Daddy!"

He spun around. Yellow braids flapping, her cheeks red, Christina was racing out of the house as fast as her short, sturdy legs would carry her. Her blue eyes were hidden by the black brim of his cowboy hat, but she had such a glorious smile on her face, it nearly broke his heart.

"Watch where you're going, sweetheart!"

When she skidded up to him, he swept her high in his arms. She wrapped her arms around his neck and locked her legs around his waist as if to never let him go.

"You forgot your hat, Daddy."

He took it from her and placed it on his head.

"Thanks, sweetheart."

"And I wanted to ask you to come for Christmas dinner."

"Well, I don't know that I can promise that. The way things stand between me and your mother, I may be going back to Alaska before—"

"Mommy's coming out to ask you, too."

Leander looked toward the big house and saw the slim, hesitant figure in a tight yellow sweater and jeans at the front door. He caught the gleam of her lovely golden hair. She'd put on lipstick, and she had her purse.

He smiled warily at Christina. "You little manipulator."

Heddy started to rush toward them, walking fast, and then she began running.

"I need to talk to your daddy alone," Heddy said breathlessly, her face prettily flushed. She did not look at him, though.

"Sure," he said offhandedly, hugging Christina tighter, not looking Heddy's way, either.

"We need to have a rational conversation. I mean, after all, we are Christina's parents," Heddy said. "Can we go somewhere?"

"Sure." He set Christina down and opened the door of his truck.

Heddy knelt and kissed the little girl goodbye and sent her back to the house to check on Cleo. Both he and Heddy watched fondly as she ran the entire way. Only when she turned and gave them a final wave before disappearing into the house, did they turn back to each other. Even then they avoided eye contact.

Lounging negligently in the lee of his open door, Leander purred lazily, "After you, Sugar."

She got in silently, and then he circled the vehicle and got in, too. For a while they drove in silence.

But the silence got to him. Big-time.

Leander pulled his black Stetson lower to shade his eyes from the glare coming off the road. To hide from Heddy, too. His stomach tightened; his throat knotted next. He grew increasingly uneasy and suspicious of Heddy as they drove toward Kinney in his truck.

She'd said they had to talk.

Yeah. Right.

Then why had she brushed against him climbing into the truck if talk was all she had on her mind?

We need to have a rational conversation.

Right. That's why she'd darkened her eyes with that blue war paint and put on blush. That's why she'd tied her hair back with a yellow ribbon and splashed herself with that flowery perfume. That's why she was wearing those skin-tight jeans that showed off her tiny waist and the curve of her hips.

I mean, after all, we are Christina's parents.

Right. Motherhood and apple pie.

That's why she'd dressed sexily, leaving several buttons of her yellow sweater undone. That's why she'd gone braless so that she could tempt him with tantalizing glimpses of her pale throat and creamy cleavage, so that every time she moved or leaned toward him, he'd be aware of her breasts.

He hadn't even touched her. Hell, he'd barely looked at her, and she had him as hard and as hot as a brick in a kiln.

Where the hell could they talk? Without her coming on to him and getting the upper hand?

I made a rational decision to go back to Alaska and divorce her.

He caught the dizzying smell of her and cursed himself for still wanting her.

Damn. Just this once he was going to do the smart thing where she was concerned.

And then he saw it—the giant vanilla ice cream cone suspended high against the cobalt blue sky, a white jet trail streaming off to one side of it.

Bingo!

Better than bingo!

Salvation!

When he braked and put on his right turn signal, she made a soft little honeyed sound of dismay.

He felt her blue eyes burning into him as she said a single desperate word. "Here?" And then when he said nothing, she pleaded, "Leander, why here?"

"You said you wanted to talk," he replied as dispassionately as he could as he swerved under the huge fake cone into Kinney's only fast-food establishment. "Besides—I'm hungry."

That was a bald-faced lie.

"What have you got against the Dairy Princess anyway?" he murmured dryly, inordinately glad his choice had so displeased her. "This used to be our favorite place when we were kids."

Another bald-faced lie. They had always preferred being alone.

"It is *the* most public place in town," she said. "Everybody comes here to talk about everybody else. Why don't we just skywrite our conversation over the town square, so everybody can read it. Or better, paint a banner and hang it from the water tower?"

"Good idea."

She scowled. He grinned.

He forced a flippant lightness into his tone. "Now you're getting the spirit of this gossip thing, Sugar. If we can't lick 'em, we'll just have to join 'em."

"What?"

Leander tossed a cynical smile toward Yates and the fat deputy in the next car, who were drinking coffee from heavy mugs. Both officers were now staring at them in bug-eyed curiosity. "Guess y'all could hear better if I rolled my window down a bit," he hollered, as he lowered his glass.

"*Leander!* Don't!" she begged as he smiled and waved at the law officers who lifted their mugs and waved back.

"I wasn't serious," she hissed.

"Everybody's been talking about us ever since we were born, Heddy. Maybe it's about time we gave 'em box seats to the show."

"Not right now. Not this afternoon. Not when—" her voice faltered "—when our marriage is at stake."

"Sugar, whoa! Let's get something straight up front—our marriage is over."

"But," Heddy began, "doesn't what Tia said change everything?"

He was grateful for the waitress's voice blasting statically from the rusty speaker under his window.

"You want anything, Sugar?" Leander asked in a disinterested tone, interrupting her, as if his primary interest was food.

"No!"

Her brows swept together as Leander hollered down at the speaker, placing an order for two burgers, three sacks of fries, a black cow, a chocolate sundae and a small root beer.

"You can't possibly eat all that!"

His eyes slid lazily over her and then away, but not before he felt an almost overpowering urge to slide his fingers inside her sweater and touch her luscious skin. He grinned in spite of himself. "You steal."

"Not today. How can you even think of food? I'm too upset to eat a single bite."

"You always say that." He stared straight ahead and then yawned, as if he were bored. "You were saying, Sugar?"

"Leander, I know the truth now. And that changes everything. For me...at least."

The soft pain in her voice cut him to the quick.

Fool, for once play it smart.

"Maybe for you, but not for me," he said harshly. "I never laid so much as a hand on your father. I always knew that. You should have, too."

"But I didn't," she said, her voice low and choked.

"Well, maybe you should have figured it out. I never, not once in my whole life, ever hurt anybody weaker or older or poorer than me. You know how I always hated bullies."

"Leander, I do know the truth now. I'm so sorry that I ever doubted you." Again that fragile sound of pain in her soft voice tore at him, because it made her seem so vulnerable and in need of his protection.

Desire for her raced along his veins and lit fires in every nerve.

Smart. Be smart. Use your brains.

"So am I," he said roughly. "But we can't undo the past."

"I love you."

God. The clincher to claw out his heart.

Smart. Be smart. Use your brains.

He stared at Yates and the deputy who were straining to hear every word.

"Yeah—till the next time you decide to turn on me." Leander's voice was as dry as dust. "You're like a ligh switch—on, off. On, off. Most of the time it's been off, Heddy."

"Not anymore," she pleaded.

"No?" He closed his eyes, so he wouldn't be so aware of her. Not that he could shut out the smell of her or the magnetic pull she exerted by just being there. But when he spoke, it was not of the present, but of past emotions he'd felt.

"You know, Heddy, I grew up loving you. Only you. Even though everybody, especially your folks, were always making me feel I wasn't good enough for you. Sometimes you were kind of snooty, too, especially when you were around Tia."

"I never meant—"

"Hey, let me finish." He waited till he was sure she was quiet. "It wasn't easy, growing up with nothing, with nobody, not even knowing my real name. But then I *had* to go and fall in love with the town goddess."

She reddened.

"Not only did everybody figure I had an ulterior motive, Sugar, but I had to learn so much—what fork to eat with, what to say in 'polite' company when some rich jerk asked me what my daddy did. I used to pore over etiquette books in the library, trying to learn all sorts of stupid rules that didn't make a lick of sense to me—just so I wouldn't embarrass you in front of Tia's fancy friends. Then you went off to those European private schools. After that you had to be a debutante. I stayed home, going to school, working my guts out just to pay bills, writing in my spare time. But most of all I went crazy with jealousy every time the gossips told me about some rich guy escorting you to one of those debutante balls. I needed you so much back then! You had everything—you didn't need me. And yet I couldn't let you go. It was the battle of my life. Every time we'd fight, I always wondered if it wouldn't really be better if we broke up. I got real real tired of it, Heddy."

"Leander—"

He held up his hand. "Hush, Sugar. Let me finish."

She sighed as he continued.

"Then after I pulled that damn fool stunt in New Orleans and we got married, I tried my damnedest to make it work. But the whole town turned against me—even you. Everybody said I married you for the ranch. Then your daddy died, and suddenly I was a murderer, too. I brought scandal to the sacred Kinney name, and you couldn't stand that. You treated me like I was less than the lowest vaquero. You—nobody else—drove me away. I can't forget that."

"I know that, Leander. And I'll never be able to forgive my—"

"Then I came back when Christina was born. The gossips told me how you nearly died having her—naturally they blamed me for that, too, of course. So did Tia. I wanted to see you so bad. I could have forgiven you everything, because I was so glad you were alive and that we had a healthy daughter, but you refused even to see me. After that, it was like something broke in me—"

"I didn't even know you came...till Tia told me in the hospital today. Oh, Leander. I'm so sorry."

"Well, it doesn't matter now. What I guess I'm trying to say is that I can't ever be sure how you'll treat me. When I came back this time, it was the same thing all over again. You were glad to see me and hot at first, chasing me down the road. And then all Tia had to do was call on the phone. You turned on me before she even had her heart attack. And then you promised her—"

"Because—"

"Look, we've spent most of our marriage apart, maybe it'd be a whole lot easier on everybody if we went on that way. I just can't take any more."

He stared past her, tight-lipped and unbiddable, not wanting to dwell on how translucently pale she looked. On how her fists were knotted weakly in her lap. On how her thick silence and despair made him feel like he was suffocating.

"What about Christina?" Heddy asked in a low desperate tone.

He hated the thought of kids suffering, especially his kid. "She'll adjust," he said harshly. "Same as half the kids in America do. Same as I did."

"She needs a father."

"Maybe you should have considered that before. Besides—she has one. It's you who won't have a husband. Leastways, not till you marry Marcus."

"But I'm not going to marry him."

"That's not what I hear. He's over at the house and with you at the hospital all the time."

"He's a friend."

"Yeah. Right." He paused. "Look, Heddy—"

A buxom waitress in a short skirt brought out the order. Leander forced himself to turn away from Heddy and to flirt and laugh with the other woman while they raised and lowered the window to get the tray attached. He put a burger, a sack of fries and the root beer on the dash where Heddy could reach them and kept the rest on the tray for himself.

When he wasn't looking he heard the paper bag on the dash crinkle as she took a fry.

"See, I told you you'd steal."

"Is...is it Mary Ann?" Heddy's voice was very small, very tight.

He was munching into mustard, onions, pickles, burned meat and a soggy bun. Food he had no appetite for. "What?"

"Is she the reason you won't give me another chance?"

He chewed thoughtfully for a while before saying, "Good Lord, no. The last thing I need is another woman working me over."

"Everybody says—"

"I thought you told Christina not to pay attention to gossip."

"You went out with her last night."

"I was helping her with her novel."

"All night? Under the water tower?"

"She's not a very skillful writer. She needed a lot of editorial advice."

"I'll bet she has other talents—"

He swore softly as he set his burger down. "No! It's not Mary Ann!"

"Then why are you dead set on going back to Alaska?"

Hell. He turned. From the deep shadow of his wide-brimmed hat, he stared straight into her beautiful blue eyes.

Which was a mistake. Because just looking at her like that always formed that soul-to-soul connection that had hooked him in the first place. Because the sunlight was shining in her hair and her yellow knit top was stretching tightly across her breasts leaving next to nothing to his imagination. And because the longer he let himself be with her, the more he felt like staying and the less he felt like going.

Smart. Be smart. Use your brains.

"'Cause I think maybe we've caused each other enough grief, Sugar."

He took a long swig of his icy black cow, praying that the cold drink would cool him down.

When she thought he wasn't watching, she snitched two more fries.

"I agree," she said softly, nibbling a juicy golden fry.

He was stunned. "You *agree?*" Odd, how his deep voice was suddenly so unsteady. He found he couldn't take his eyes off that fry disappearing inch by inch inside her pink lips.

"Yes," she breathed, sucking in the last of that fry. "I think it's time we gave each other joy." She licked the salty tip of her second fry.

"Whoa!" He drew in a harsh breath and slammed his black cow down on the dash, sloshing foam all over the top of the mug. "It's been so long, I wouldn't know where to begin," he said, mopping the mess with a wad of paper napkins.

"But I do." She scooted nearer, reaching for him.

"Heddy—" he said hoarsely.

But she buried her face in the hollow of his neck. Every muscle in his body bunched when her tongue flicked across the base of his throat.

Leander strangled a curse. "What the hell do you think you're doing now, Sugar?"

She lifted her beautiful gaze to his, but she didn't speak. She didn't have to.

Through thick, downcast lashes her jewel blue eyes blazed softly with love—for him. Her slim fingers curled tighter into his chest. A warm, staccato breath of air escaped her lips and feathered across his, causing every male sensory receptor in his body to come alive, as little frissons of desire raced along his heated nerve ends.

Damn those eyes of hers, for making him know how starved he was for her. Damn her lithe sensual female beauty. With a supreme effort he willed himself to resist her.

"What am I doing?" she whispered silkily. "Just the same thing you did that night in New Orleans when you won me in that card game. You fought for me that night, Leander. You were poor and drunk and scared, but you came to that posh hotel and gambled against incredible odds. You knew I was making a mistake, and that we would both be miserable. Then you married me. You were good to my family, and we were terrible to you. Well, you're not poor anymore. Nobody's ever going to say you came back to me for the ranch." A beat passed. "I've made my mistakes... lots of them. I've hurt you. So has my family. But I'm sorry. If you leave me now, when we might finally have a chance to be happy, you'll be making the worst mistake of all."

Her words touched him; he felt a wave of emotion stronger than any he'd ever known. For days he hadn't been able to get her touch, her smell, the heat and shape of her body out of his mind.

But it wasn't enough. Not if he couldn't trust her. Not if she would just go back to her old ways.

His voice was rough, he pushed her hands away. "That's a crock of horse—"

He would have opened his door and gotten out, but she moved faster than quicksilver. Her mouth fastened over his, devouring his swearword in one last desperate attempt to change his mind.

Quiet tears filled her eyes and beaded her lashes.

"*Please,* Leander. *Oh, please—*"

Her plea seemed wrenched from her tender soul in those final seconds before her soft mouth seized his again. "Please, give me another chance."

He inhaled the dizzying scent of her perfume. Golden clouds of sweet-smelling hair foamed silkily against his cheek and throat. The instant she fused her gentle mouth to his and he tasted her, pleasure and desire saturated his body.

He wanted to believe her. He wanted to so desperately.

Smart. Be smart.

But she was kissing him in a frenzy of hope and despair, and his brain short-circuited.

He had no illusions as to their future happiness. But her lips were molten hot as her soft body melted into his.

When her hands moved over the corded muscles of his shoulders, kneading and then tightening as a passionate little moan of ecstasy escaped her lips, she set him aflame.

A shudder went through him. Her moist velvet tongue dipped into his mouth and he was lost.

His hands began to move down her body, gently exploring, as he molded her flush against himself. Soon he forgot everything except the familiar pleasure of touching her and kissing her, and she withheld nothing, surrendering herself with a wild, reckless abandon. Every single day since he'd had her that night, he'd craved her.

He had no sensation of time or place or of their avidly fascinated audience as he pulled her onto his lap and washed her throat and nape with his tongue. He had no sensation of anything except the exquisite rapture she aroused. He began to shake. More than anything he wanted to make fierce, wild love to her.

Then dimly, very dimly at first, Yates's voice penetrated Leander's bedazzled consciousness.

"What are they doing now? Did you see that? *Hot damn!*" A veritable yelp of pain, followed by howls and curses, erupted from Yates's car.

"Bill! This coffee's boiling!" Yates was bellowing now, squirming to unzip his slacks. "Get me a towel! Get me a damn waitress! Quick! Myrtle! Over here, girl! Your damn tray fell in my lap!"

"Da—amn," Leander muttered in broken syllables. "Damn." Reluctantly Leander kissed the golden curls on her forehead as he gently began easing her off himself. "Heddy, Sugar..."

"Mmmmm." Her beautiful blue eyes were feverish and confused.

He traced his callused hand through her tangled hair. "Sugar, er...I...we've got to stop...for now."

"Why?" she asked, her tone soft and slurred with desire as she attempted to kiss his bottom lip searingly again.

"No...Sugar, look over there. Yates and that lard-of-fat deputy of his and damned near everybody else in Kinney are watching us."

"So?" She looped her arms loosely around his neck and kissed his mouth again. "You were the one who wanted to give them box seats."

He strummed her hair back behind her ears and cupped her chin lovingly. "I changed my mind, Sugar. This definitely has to be a private showing."

Ten

They were in his cabin, and the fire he had lit made a flickering orange glow against the stone walls and wooden floors. Not that either of them needed a fire, Heddy thought unsteadily. The sexual tension sizzling between them, ever since they'd kissed at the Dairy Princess, was as hot and dangerously electric as a live wire.

And now at last—she had him alone.

It was a good thing she'd told her housekeeper she might be out all night, she thought, as she went to his stereo and put on a compact disc. In an instant a wild, haunting love song washed over them.

She felt the magnetic pull of Leander's burning black eyes as she turned toward him. The warm flush that ran through her body was terrifying in its intensity.

Still wearing his hat and jeans and boots, he lay sprawled across his bed, staring at her as if she were already naked.

"Strip," he ordered in an uneven whisper.

Her heart was beating too fast and too loudly, as she shyly began to pace the small room. Her ribs felt squeezed, and she kept taking deep breaths.

This was her chance. Her one final chance to win him. She could run.

Or she could play it for all it was worth.

A quietness fell over her that had nothing to do with the wild melody.

When she began to undulate, slowly at first, to the beat of the music, Leander tensed, stretching his frame like a panther before he forced himself to relax again.

His eyes never left her face as she reached above her head and languidly untied the yellow ribbon in her hair, so that the loose silken waves fell down around her shoulders in a cascade of golden flame. "Throw me your hat, cowboy," she whispered.

He cocked the brim back from his forehead with his thumb and then, with a practiced flick of his wrist, he caught hold of the edge and sailed it to her like a Frisbee.

She caught it and put it on—slowly, slanting it at a rakish angle.

Then she lowered her hands over her body, sliding them down her hips, slowly running them back up her waist over her silky smooth breasts to the buttons of her yellow sweater as she swayed provocatively to the beat of the music.

A muscle ticked savagely along his jawline as he stared fixedly at her from beneath his heavy black lashes.

"Take it off—cowgirl," he drawled in a husky timbre. "Take it all off."

She felt dizzy, strange. But she said teasingly in a trembly voice, "Can I leave your hat on?"

He nodded with an enthrallingly intimate smile.

She moved closer to the fire, and with deft, quick fingers, undid each tiny yellow button, moving and twisting, causing firelight and shadow to flicker across her body. Slowly, very slowly, she released the last pearly button from its buttonhole.

As she peeled the edges of yellow wool apart to reveal a strip of honeyed skin, he gasped expectantly. But just as the gap widened to give him more than a tantalizing glimpse of her breasts, she turned the slim curve of her back to him and slipped her sweater down so that it fell halfway off her shoulders.

"Turn back around," he commanded quietly.

For a long moment she hesitated—teasing him instead with the slender curve of her naked spine instead.

Then suddenly she whirled and faced him again. She cocked his Stetson at a more coquettish angle. With her lashes downcast and her head held back, her fiery hair tumbled down her back. She planted both hands on her hips in a seductive pose and thrust her breasts forward. In that swift fluid gesture the sweater that had been clinging to the jutting tips of her soft pink nipples succumbed to gravity and fell from her body to the floor.

"Come over here, Sugar." This time his voice was deep and very gentle. And very hot. As hot as the fire warming the bare skin of her back.

She stepped daintily over the pool of yellow wool. "But I haven't taken off my jeans."

His black eyes glittered.

She slipped her fingertips down her abdomen and then beneath her frayed denim waistband, unsnapping the single metal button. Then slowly she inched the zipper down, so that her partially opened jeans exposed a resplendent V of rosy flesh above her sex.

Her graceful young body, thus revealed, twirled closer to him, and then retreated.

"Heddy—"

She began pushing her jeans down, rotating her hips from the waist, undulating with the wanton expertise of a natural; instinctively knowing just how to sway that which would most excite him.

"Come here, damn you!"

Startled, she disobeyed on a nervous giggle, undressing more slowly.

When her jeans lay beside her sweater, she wore nothing but his black hat and a pair of minuscule black lace bikini panties. The flickering firelight played across her tawny skin and glimmered in her hair.

"Where the hell did you learn to do that?" he groaned.

"Nowhere. You are the only man I've ever had, Leander." Slowly she closed her eyes and danced to the hypnotic tempo of the passionate music, deliberately arousing him. "There has never been anyone but you."

Her voice was a honeyed caress; her innocent face glowed like an angel. But it was the wanton invitation in her brilliant blue eyes as she opened them that sent him over that fatal edge.

In a single leap he was off the bed and she was crushed in his powerful arms. Shoving her against the stone wall, he tore his hat off her head and pitched it to the wooden floor.

She had confessed that there had never been anyone but him. For all his passion, she felt a fleeting sadness that he did not make the same oath to her.

But the hard, hot feel of his hands moving over her naked flesh rocked her senses. The musky scent of him enveloped her. He caught her wrists and raised them above her head and caught her in a passionate embrace. Slowly his hand traced down the length of her arms. Then his fingers grasped the thick golden coils of hair at the nape of her neck and forced her head back. With ruthless mastery he pressed bruising kisses on her lips, her throat, her breasts.

Breathing hard, he savagely wrenched his jeans and shirt off, stripping out of his clothes with a great deal more haste than she had. Then he forced her back against the cool stone wall, parting her thighs with his leg, his hands sliding under her hips, cupping her, positioning her, lifting her around his waist. With her spine against cool stone, her legs locked around his back and her arms around his neck, he drove into her.

"Ah, Heddy. My beautiful Heddy—"

If he was wild for her, he made her wilder. Crying out softly, she gloried in all the sensual pleasures of their lovemaking—in the way his breathing had roughened, marveling at the heated textures of his bronze sculpted muscles moving against her softer flesh. She ran her hands over his ribbed chest that was thickly carpeted with black hair, savoring his masculine beauty. As always his skin grew increasingly hot, and soon her own temperature rose.

A warm blush of color spread across her pale skin, tinting her cheeks, her throat, her breasts, but she would not let him linger at any point. The rapidly increasing beat of her pulse raced in tempo with his. He drove into her again and again. When she began to shudder and moan, returning his kisses wantonly, he lost all control. Feverishly in that last moment before the cataclysm, he fused his mouth to hers in a final long hot kiss.

"Heddy. Ah, Heddy," he groaned as he began to shudder.

Afterward, she felt drained and faint from the pleasure, too dizzy even to stand. So he picked her up in his arms and carried her to the bed. They lay down together, and she curled against his body, nestling there until she fell asleep in the warmth of his arms. Later they woke and showered, lathering each other with soap, making love again against the tiles while they were still wet and slick.

Once more they showered and made love again until all the hot water was gone.

The next time, he took her on the floor by the fire with his lips and tongue. As she did him. His body heat was at his usual high, and she found this sort of sex exquisitely delicious.

He drew the infinitely tender, profoundly intimate, process out until her whole body seemed a mass of nerve endings all quivering for release. Until she felt hotter and closer to him and more cherished by him than ever before. Still, he made her hover on that titillating edge of erotic delight for hours. Then he satisfied her with a single deft flick of his warm tongue which sent spirals of pleasure radiating throughout her limbs. And when he finished, she was left with the pleasant salty aftertaste of him lingering in her mouth. Afterward she felt so utterly sated and tenderhearted as she lay beside him that she wept from the sheer beauty of it.

Beside them in the hearth, the fire had dwindled to glowing coals. Above them the misshapen antler chandelier loomed.

He pulled her golden head into the curve of his shoulder and draped his arm over her. She lay in the darkness and reveled in her newfound happiness, believing that at last she had made him know that she truly loved him, believing that he had to love her in return.

But he dispelled that illusion with a casual sentence or two, thanking her for the good time.

She blushed miserably, longing for words that would betray the depth of his love and give spiritual meaning to the act.

When he said no more, she whispered gently, "I love you. For me . . . it wasn't just sex. It never could be. Not with you."

"Wasn't it?" he murmured darkly, getting up then.

"Leander—"

"Don't start!" His voice cracked like a spark, across the firelit darkness. "Tonight was good." He yanked on his jeans but didn't snap them. "Too good." Next he shrugged into his shirt. "Let's leave it at that."

"But, I can't."

"Sure you can, Sugar."

"Leander, *please*—"

A muscle jumped convulsively at the corner of his mouth. His shirt unbuttoned, the edges of it hanging apart to reveal a strip of dark brown muscles, he got back in bed beside her. "Shhh."

"But—"

"Shhh. I can't bear it." He smiled so tightly that white lines radiated about the edges of his lips. When she tried to tell him again how she felt, he kissed her into silence.

She began to touch him, caressing his naked skin beneath his open shirt with shaking fingertips. He shuddered but remained tense, his passion toward her under control now.

Frustrated that he would neither make love nor talk, she finally gave up and lay still. It was enough that he was beside her. Surely he would listen when she tried to explain in the morning. She lay her head on his pillow and let herself drowsily succumb to the drugging bliss of his blazing warmth. She couldn't expect miracles overnight.

Her last sleepy thoughts were about how good he was with the children, even Attilla. About how thrilled Christina would be when she told her that her father was staying.

Heddy fell asleep, certain of their reconciliation. In the morning she would make him eggs and coffee like a real wife. She would tell him how much she loved him. He would listen and smile. Perhaps he still wouldn't quite believe. But she couldn't expect him to trust her immediately. It would take time, but she had time. She had the rest of their lives.

Heddy was determined to make up to Leander for all the hurt she had unintentionally caused him. She would nurture him, adore him, spoil him—in bed as well as out of it. And someday he would have to forgive her and come to love her again as he had in the past. As she loved him.

She was sure that at last, everything was going to be wonderful between them.

She slept so soundly she did not hear him get up in the night.

The next morning she woke up gradually, perceiving in her first hazy moment of consciousness only that she was bathed in the golden warmth of sunlight. Then languidly she stirred and reached toward his pillow, her heart filled with the warmth and love she wanted to bestow upon him.

Instead of silky black hair, her fingers brushed a hard, felt hat brim.

Startled, she jumped up and stared at the black Stetson lying in the indentation where only hours before Leander's head had been.

Where was he?

In a panic she saw that his suitcases and laptop were gone. Frantically she wrapped a sheet around herself and ran to the porch. Jim Bob's truck was gone, too.

Oaks and mesquite stood like silent sentinels. Not a breath of air stirred through their leafless branches. High above her a solitary buzzard made lazy circles.

The stillness and the quiet settled oppressively upon her spirit.

She was all alone. Leander had left her.

Feeling desolate, she wandered aimlessly back inside. Shakily she went to the bed and lifted the black Stetson from the pillow.

A single white slip of paper fluttered to the floor and landed beside her discarded yellow sweater and jeans.

For a long moment she was afraid to pick it up. When she did, she sobbed when she saw that his note was for Christina, and not her.

Heddy stared at the black swirls of ink, her mind a disbelieving blank.

The words ran together in an unintelligible blur as she began to read. Only with great effort did she manage to focus.

He told Christina he'd left his hat behind for her, so that she could wear it whenever she missed him. But that she had to let Attilla and Cleo take turns wearing it. He said he'd left Christmas presents for her and the other children under their "Cowboy Christmas" tree. He invited her to come to Alaska for the summer. He promised her a long letter explaining why he had to divorce her mother.

Divorce?

When Heddy saw that he had not written a single word to her, not even goodbye, despair opened before her like a chasm.

Eleven

Forsaken.

For the first time in her life Heddy felt completely alone.
Completely abandoned.

Even though she was surrounded by people.

She had been a foolish, vain creature who had overestimated her desirability. She had also overestimated Leander's ability to forgive her for not standing by him when he'd needed her. For more than eight years she had let Tia persuade her to doubt Leander and thereby had condemned him to exile. She was sorry now, sorrier than she'd ever been for anything.

Somehow she worked, putting in long days at her busy shop, selling and wrapping Christmas presents. Somehow she found time to visit Tia and care for the children. She cooked and told bedtime stories. She showed endless items to exasperating last-minute shoppers, but she existed in a numb, zombielike state.

Mommy, you're not listening!

Heddy, dear, would you bring me my walker?

For the third time, do you, or do you not, have this red blouse with the cute little ruffles down the front in a size twelve?

Someone was always demanding something of her.

But she was only half there.

Leander didn't call.

He didn't write.

Not even to Christina who jumped as she herself did every time the phone rang, who raced down the long black-topped drive every afternoon wearing his cowboy hat to check their rural mailbox for a letter.

The tension inside Heddy mounted until finally one morning as she folded a sexy nightie in tissue for an embarrassed husband in a black Stetson who was shopping for a wife he obviously adored, she burst into tears. Tossing the nightie and gift box on the counter in front of Mary Ann, Heddy raced out of the shop.

She couldn't put the beauty of her last night with Leander out of her mind—when she had tried to show him how completely she loved him. When she had thought he had showed her the same thing. After such shared intimacies, some part of Heddy marveled that Leander could coldly walk out on her.

And yet some part of her understood.

Once he had tried to describe his feelings for the woman who had given birth to him and then left him in a garbage Dumpster to die. He had wanted to know what kind of coldhearted monster could give birth and then throw her own baby away.

"I used to dream about her when I lived in those awful foster homes. She was always beautiful—like an angel. She would come back for me and I would be so happy to see her at first. Then I would ask her, 'Why did you leave me? Why didn't you love me?' I always woke up before she answered. And you know something—I was always glad I did.

"She was *my* mother," he had said, "and I loved her and wanted her, no matter what she'd done. But at the same time I was glad she never came back for me, because I wouldn't have trusted her, and I was afraid that I might be like her."

As a boy Leander had possessed a vein of ice in him that enabled him to withdraw into himself and reject people. She had seen him do it with the bullies at school and with Tia's snooty friends. It was a survival technique he'd learned in those first bitterly lonely years of his childhood before Mrs. Janovich had adopted him. Now Heddy wondered if he wasn't doing the same thing to her.

Was he afraid of her love? Was he afraid of getting in too deep and losing her again? Or was he capable of turning his emotions off the same way his own mother had when she'd left him to die?

Maybe Leander could survive alone. Maybe he could survive without their love. But Heddy knew she couldn't. Not again.

Maybe he thought he could use her for a wild, wonderful night of soul-shattering sex, and then pack his bags, and go back to Alaska. Maybe he was even trying to get even.

Heddy didn't blame him. But understanding his possible reasons didn't lessen the hurt.

After Christina read her Leander's note, she'd cried, "This is all your fault, Mommy!"

"No—"

"Yes!" she'd screamed, tears streaming down her cheeks. "Everyone in Kinney says so!"

Christina ran to her room and locked herself inside, refusing to answer Heddy when she pleaded with her through the door. The next morning a pale, red-eyed Christina emerged. Sweeping down the stairs, she avoided her mother, choosing to hold court instead on the huge flowered couch in the parlor where she shared her father's note with Cleo and Attilla. Attilla who had trouble concentrating except on his very favorite stories, made her read it three times.

Then the children solemnly marched into the library. There they tore through the drawers of the ormolu escritoire to get stamps and stationery and pencils so they could write Leander—even Attilla, who could barely sit still, much less hold a pencil and concentrate on one thing long enough to write a letter. Nevertheless, in between grinding three pencils down to their nubs and jamming the electric pencil sharpener and then spilling pencil shavings all over the carpet, he laboriously managed two lines, a postscript, at the bottom of Christina's letter—"Come back soon, Uncle Pepper. We miss you lots."

A day or so later Tia came home from the hospital, but she was so weak and breathless, a hospital bed had to be set up downstairs. Ironically, as soon as Heddy finished arranging her pillows, the old lady demanded to see Leander.

For a long moment Heddy just stared at her, not believing what she was hearing.

"Well then, where is your impossible husband?" Tia demanded restlessly.

An immense weariness of spirit engulfed Heddy. "He's . . . gone, Tia. Back to Alaska."

"When did this happen?"

"A few days ago."

"Why didn't anyone tell me?"

"I—I just couldn't, Tia."

"You'll have to speak louder. I seem to be having trouble hearing."

"I—I said, I just couldn't."

"Well then, what are you going to do about it?"

"Nothing."

"That doesn't sound like you."

"I—I thought you hated him, Tia."

"Well, I suppose...I do," Tia declared but without much of her former conviction. "But..." Her voice quavered. "The ranch could use a man to run things...at least while I'm down. Not that I won't be up and around by spring."

"Of course you will be."

"Then there's Attilla. Give him another year or two, and you'll never be able to manage him without a man."

"Leander is gone, Tia. For good."

"I thought you loved him."

"What's love got to do with it?"

Heddy hired round-the-clock nurses and therapists to care for Tia. Even so, when Heddy was home, it was Heddy's attention that the difficult old lady constantly demanded. And much to her surprise Tia badgered her incessantly to go after Leander.

Heddy couldn't eat. Or sleep. She couldn't bear the thought of Christmas without Leander. Nor could she think of her approaching birthday without bursting into tears. She couldn't turn the radio on in her car because the Christmas music made her feel even sadder. Finally she left her shop in Mary Ann's hands because everything there reminded her of Christmas.

Even the children lost their joy in the holiday. They were angrier at Santa Claus than they were at her.

"Why are you mad at Santa Claus?" Heddy asked when they rebelled in the grocery store, refusing to let her buy chocolate chip cookie ingredients because they weren't going to bake any cookies on Christmas Eve for Santa.

"Not a single cookie!" Attilla swore vehemently, throwing the package of chocolate chips back on the shelf.

For a long moment his freckled hand lingered on the package, as if he was sorely tempted to put it back in the shopping cart when nobody was watching. He adored stuffing himself on cookies almost as much as he adored making mischief.

Christina crossed her arms across her chest. "If Santa really was very magic, he would have made my daddy stay in Texas. Santa has been very bad this year, and he doesn't deserve a cookie."

"He's too fat, anyway," Cleo said, not to be left out.

"Let's leave him switches," Attilla suggested, "'cause that's what you're always saying he'll leave me if I'm bad."

Anytime they were all home and the phone rang, Heddy and the children would race to get it, hoping it would be Leander.

Then one bright sunny morning, while she and Tia were making out the final grocery list for their Christmas dinner, a lawyer called and said he had been hired to represent Leander in the divorce.

"But...but I don't want to divorce my husband," Heddy had whispered into the phone as the three children and Tia hung on her every word. "The situation is—" Heddy's voice cracked.

"Unremediable, I am afraid. You see, Mrs. Knight, my client wants to divorce you as soon as possible."

Sunlight streamed into the yellow-papered kitchen as a thin-faced Heddy, her three unusually quiet children and Tia sat tensely around the table. That morning there were no sounds other than the burble of the coffee maker, an occasional spoon clinking against china, or the slurps of a child's mouth wet-vacuuming the very last drop of orange juice from his glass.

Attilla turned off his suction hose and banged his empty glass down with a vengeance. "It's nearly Christmas. We have to go get *him*."

All eyes locked on Attilla's freckled nose to which a toast crumb clung. Everybody knew who *he* was.

"Oh, dear," said Tia, seeing all the pale, unhappy faces. "Oh, dear."

Heddy set her coffee cup down very carefully. "How, Attilla? *He* is in Alaska."

"We..." Attilla grew silent and sucked in his bottom lip thoughtfully. After a long moment of intense concentration during which he amazed everybody by licking his nose clean with the tip of his curled tongue, he burst out with an idea. "We could take a rocket or a missile or maybe a jet to Alaska! We could whoosh up there, get him and bring him back!" Attilla turned his hand into a jet and made impressive blasting-off sounds with his talented tongue. "Or... maybe we could call him on the telephone. Maybe he's just sulking the way Christina does when she wants us to beg her to do something. Maybe if we talked to him real nice and said *please*—"

Christina, who was shoveling eggs into her mouth with obscene amounts of grape jelly, nearly choked. "I don't either sulk!"

"Do, too," Cleo affirmed matter-of-factly, twirling a bacon strip. "Can I ride on the tail of the rocket, Aunt Heddy?"

"I say we go up there and bring Uncle Pepper back," Attilla said, making rocket sounds again.

There was a moment of charged silence, unbroken by the clinks of spoons or the vacuuming slurps of orange juice.

Heddy felt an attack of conscience as the children stared at her with round, expectant eyes, as if Attilla's off-the-wall suggestion really was the solution.

Despite the warm sunlight streaming across the table, she shivered. "But he doesn't want me." Lamely she added, "Besides, kids, we don't have a missile."

"Then you can get one!" Tia pulled herself up until she was sitting as stiffly erect in her wheelchair as a displeased queen. "I expected more from my granddaughter!"

"More?" Heddy repeated in stricken amazement. "I threw myself at him... and he left me."

"Because he's as stubborn as we are. It's hard to back down, Heddy. Believe me," she added quietly, "I know. You get an idea in your head . . . but never mind. People fly in planes to Alaska every day of the week! It's almost your birthday, Heddy. Dear! It's almost Christmas. I remember another Christmas when you and Pepper set this town on its ear."

"You mean when he won me playing poker on my wedding night and we eloped to Mexico?" Heddy flushed hot pink.

"Maybe it's time you acted like a Kinney and made a real play for him. Do something wild. Take the bull by the horns. Go after him, dear. Unless you want to lose him."

"Yahoo!" Attilla whooped. Then he folded his paper napkin into a rocket with lopsided wings and pitched it high into the air.

Ivak lay on the wooden floor beside his master's heavy boots, the tip of his tail flicking tensely as he pretended to sleep. In reality he was watching Leander through his narrowly slitted topaz eyes.

Muz's half-empty bottle of whiskey stood at the ready— beside Leander's empty shot glass.

"Would you like some biscuits and tea?" Mara asked gently. "It's getting dark. You might need a little something to warm you before you set out for your cabin."

As if tea or biscuits could warm him. As if anything in the whole damn world could warm him except—

Leander saw golden hair fanning over his pillow. A tawny body with curved hips undulating before a flickering fire. He saw Heddy wearing nothing except his black cowboy hat. He saw her lips parting in a seductive smile.

Leander shook his head and reached blindly across the table for another cigarette. When he found the package empty, he wadded it up and pitched it toward the trash can. Mara picked it up when he missed.

As he leaned forward he peered glumly through the ice-encrusted window. The dim light was fading into darkness fast. Too fast. The night would be long and fiercely cold. And dark. He needed to go home before the last of the light went. Instead he got up and bummed another pack of cigarettes from Muz.

Leander had quit smoking when he was eighteen.

He had a headache from too many cigarettes and too little sleep.

Leander avoided liquor because it opened him up to the bleak feelings of loneliness and abandonment he'd had to fight ever since his childhood.

Yet when he stomped into Muz's cabin early this morning, as he had every morning since he'd returned to Alaska, and reached over the counter for Muz's bottle, he had told himself just one small shot—just to get him over the headache from another sleepless night and too many cigarettes. Muz had reminded him he'd used the same line yesterday.

But one drink had made the headache worse. So had two. He had four more drinks and dozens of cigarettes to get him through the morning.

Somewhere after the sixth shot, he'd stopped counting; his headache was no better, but he'd stopped caring.

"Mara, tell Muz to call Juneau. I want two cases of whiskey and cigarettes sent up here on the next mail plane."

"You're killing yourself," Mara said from the kitchen.

"So, the hell, what."

Leander heard her footsteps padding toward him. Not that he looked up as Mara pulled out a chair and sat down beside him. "Do you want to tell me what happened in Texas?"

He drew a deep shuddering breath. "Not really. I'm getting a divorce. That's all. And, no, I don't want to talk about it."

"Maybe you should think about it then."

He fell silent.

"The decision to divorce her doesn't seem to be making you very happy. The fact is, it's killing you."

His morose black eyes impaled her with shards of ice.

"I'm divorcing her. And that's final. She turned on me one time too many—just like my mother—"

"Just like—"

"Hell, just leave me alone," he snapped.

Everything was oppressive to him—the gray skies, the snow, the long black nights, and even Mara's pretty hurt face, which reminded him of Heddy. Most of all he felt oppressed by the utter aloneness he now experienced without Heddy. Not that he shouldn't be used to it by now.

Why the hell had he gone back to Texas, anyway?

What had he been trying to prove? If he hadn't gone, he would never have known for sure what he had lost. Seeing Heddy again had opened him to the pain, even worse than the booze did.

He got up and yanked his parka off the peg.

"I know I've been hard to take. Don't worry. I won't be back," he said. "Not till that mail plane gets in with my whiskey and cigarettes Saturday. I've gotta handle this alone."

Alone. The feeling smothered him and froze him like the great lonely cold.

All his life he'd been alone.

Even though he was rich and famous, for the rest of his life he'd be alone.

He kissed Mara goodbye and stepped outside into bleak, wintry, bone-freezing whiteness with Ivak trotting faithfully along behind him.

He threw his long leg across the seat of his snowmobile, smiling grimly when the image of flying the little machine off a cliff or smashing it into a rock flickered in his imagination.

No more pain.

No more fame. No more hassles.

No more aloneness.

He started the engine.

The minute he was out of the village, some self-destructive impulse in him screamed for more speed.

Leaning forward, his whole body charged with the vibrations, he pushed the snowmobile for all it was worth until he was flying way too fast through the bone-numbing cold. He skidded wildly down an embankment onto the ice and snow of the frozen river that wound through the forest the short distance to his cabin. For a brief moment Leander lost himself in the exhilaration of pure speed as he blasted through a huge snow drift that normally he would have avoided.

Snow and ice exploded, showering him. The wind cut through his parka.

He was cold. Too cold.

Ice was forming all over him, on his parka, his gloves, even on his eye lashes.

Faster.

He hit the slick ice and skidded wildly. He raced up a drift, and for several seconds he and the snowmobile were airborne—an out-of-control rocket flying into the blackening sky.

Then the snowmobile hit the ice heavily, lurching, nearly rolling. And then he got control.

Not that he slowed the speeding machine.

He held on to the handlebars, so cold now he was numb and shaking, and pushed the thing faster than ever.

Hell, maybe he did have a death wish.

Right now he just wanted to end the pain.

"Did you hear that Heddy Kinney chartered a Lear jet to go to Alaska and fetch Pepper?"

"No!"

"You can see it from the highway—just settin' parked out there, plain as day on the ranch runway."

"She's taking all three kids. Attilla's even got himself a rope. He says he's gonna lasso and hog-tie his Uncle Pepper and bring him home where he belongs."

"It's about time Heddy came to her senses."

"About time Pepper came to his."

"But it was terrible the way Heddy didn't stand behind him when Barret died. The way the press made him seem so spooky and mean."

"I knew all the time Pepper was innocent."

"So did I. So did everybody."

"What's Tia got to say about it?"

"The jet was her idea. She said it was her Christmas present and birthday present to both of them."

"Times change."

"For the better sometimes."

"Hey, did you hear that the city's floating a bond to paint the water tower?"

"About time."

"Like a lot of things."

The early-morning sky was a purple dome above a broken land that seemed from the mail plane to be endless ice and snow. A mountain loomed to one side of the tiny shuddering plane, its jagged face scarred with naked rock and broken trees that marked the monstrous path of a recent avalanche.

There was a strong crosswind. The plane flew at an angle fighting the wind with the bright blade of its propeller.

"You're lucky as hell, little lady, that we can even get in today," the bearded pilot with the parrot's beak nose yelled over the roar of his engine. "All our airplanes have been grounded for the better part of a week—till today. Too dangerous to fly."

"Too dangerous?" Heddy was gripping the edges of her chair as the plane jounced in the nearly constant turbulence. "But... it's safe... today?"

"It's great. A few bumps maybe."

The plane hit a pocket of nothingness and plunged.

"Yahoo!" Attilla cried, rocking back and forth in his seat, urging the plane down faster, loving it.

"That boy of yours is a natural-born pilot!"

"Are we going to crash, Aunt Heddy?" Cleo asked quietly, hiding her eyes.

"No, scaredy," Christina snapped imperiously as the plane leveled out. "We're going to get my daddy!"

"We've had nothing but weeks of pea-soup fog, black ice, and blizzards," the pilot explained.

The vibrating walls of the plane were eggshell thin. Heddy and the children were cold in spite of their heavy ski clothes. Nevertheless, Attilla's nose was glued to the icy window even though it was too fogged to see much.

"You can't tell it now, but it's pretty here in the summer," the pilot yelled. "Lots of creeks and forests and alpine meadows. The forest is alive with bears..."

"Bears!" Cleo gasped, opening her eyes, her pupils dilating until they were huge. "Are bears nice?"

"I wouldn't want to tango with 'em, hon. Here we go!" the pilot yelled spotting a clearing between the trees. "Hang on to your britches, babies. It always gets a little bumpy getting into the village."

A little bumpy... If ever there was an understatement.

For the next five minutes the pilot was totally absorbed in landing the plane. Every time he banked, Heddy's nails clawed the armrests as the small aircraft bucked like a bronco through wind shears and air pockets. Her ragged nails were still digging in long after they'd slid smoothly to a stop on the icy runway.

When they were on the ground and the pilot had shut the engine down, Attilla was in her face, his green eyes alive with feverish excitement. "Can we do it again?"

Cleo was whining, "Aunt Heddy, Attilla hid my shoes. And I have to find 'em. 'Cause I want to walk back to Texas."

Muz's phones and radios had been dead all morning, so it was impossible to reach Leander by radio. Muz had kindly offered to lend Heddy his snowmobile despite Mara's protests.

"Hell, he's been here practically every day till today," Muz explained impatiently to Heddy. "He didn't say nothing about any wife coming for Christmas. In fact he said just—"

"Muz—" Mara warned gently. "Heddy, I could tell Pepper missed you. He came into the village every day like he couldn't stand being alone out in his cabin."

Muz gave his wife a long look, and she answered it with an equally eloquent silence, defeating him in a curious battle of wills. Surrendering, Muz sat back down grumpily in front of his racks of radio equipment and put on a headset. He shook his shaggy head in frustration. "Dead as a dodo!" He pounded a fist on the counter. "What good is this stuff when it's out just when you really need it?"

"That's okay," Heddy said. "It's not your fault. I know you tried. I'm just so grateful you said you'd loan me your snowmobile."

"I really think you should go with her, Muz," Mara coaxed. "It's clear, but it's awfully cold. You know how fast the weather can change—"

"I have ridden snowmobiles lots of times when I've gone skiing in Colorado."

"But Muz knows the way," Mara persisted.

"You said it wasn't far. From the map it looks very easy to get there," Heddy said, rolling Muz's map back up.

"Believe me, in the snow, when you're out there alone, it's harder," Mara said.

"It's just a straight shot up the river," Muz repeated for the third time. "She'd have to be an idiot to miss it. And like I said, the kids can spend the day with Lori at her school. Mrs. Asuluk, their teacher, is having them clean the room and then they're having that Christmas party."

"You are all so sweet," Heddy said gratefully.

"Pepper's been our best friend for nearly eight years," Mara said. "We know how thrilled he'll be to see you."

I hope, Heddy prayed.

The weather had been clear when Heddy had zoomed out of the village on Muz's snowmobile.

But gray clouds had formed, and it was snowing now. These light flurries were accompanied by sharp frozen winds, and the falling snow made it difficult to see through the fringe of trees that lined the bank of the river. The cold numbed her muscles, especially those in her hands, and made it more difficult to control the snowmobile.

Not only that, but the river was more narrow and circuitous than Muz had led her to believe. Afraid she'd miss Leander's cabin, she kept a constant eye over her right shoulder. Which made it impossible to pay close enough attention to where she was going.

Thick snowdrifts and logs on the frozen river were a constant hazard and had to be dodged.

Crouching forward, she raced on through the freezing cold.

It seemed to be taking longer to get to Leander's cabin than Muz's map had led her to believe. She was constantly thinking that his cabin would be around the next turn. And then the next.

But it never was.

The sky was darkening, and it was growing harder and harder to see. Her adrenaline began to pump as she considered frightening possibilities. What if she had ridden past his cabin and was speeding into empty wilderness? What if she got lost in the dark?

Then she rounded the next curve and saw a light in the trees. And smoke curling.

In the next instant the light and smoke weren't there.

Had they just been illusions?

She slowed the snowmobile and struggled to focus, but the snow was falling too thickly for her to see much.

She was straining over her shoulder so hard that she didn't see the mountainous snowdrift and logjam in front of her. Not until her snowmobile slammed into them.

Snow and rocks and ice and wood erupted. The snowmobile spun crazily, and her hands were too numb to hold on to the handlebars. When she fell, the snowmobile skidded off on its own toward the embankment.

Her head struck the ice as her unmanned snowmobile crashed into a tree.

She lay in the snow, too dazed by the force of her fall to get up.

The snow fell thicker. Vaguely she felt the sharp, icy wind and the cold seeping up from the frozen river, piercing her thick ski clothes, chilling her to the bone.

At first she was afraid. Then she began to feel very sleepy. She closed her eyes, intending to lie there just for a minute, until she felt stronger.

She had read somewhere that one should dig a hole in the snow to keep warm. But her head ached. When she tried to sit up, her muscles were too numb to obey the command of her brain.

She had been so determined to reach the cabin, she hadn't realized she was so cold.

A great weariness settled upon her as the snow swirled thickly around her. The sky was almost black now. The frigid temperature of the ice numbed her brain as it did her body, lessening her terror, weakening her instincts for survival, making her feel incredibly lethargic.

Vaguely she realized that it was her birthday. And Leander's too. And that Christmas was the next day.

Her last thoughts before she fell asleep were of Leander. She heard a sound and opened her eyes.

Was someone shouting her name?

She cried out softly, but her faint voice was lost in the wind.

For a moment she thought she saw him standing above her in the snow. He was holding out two presents. "Happy birthday. Merry Christmas, Sugar. I love you. I love you."

She had come so far to hear him say those words.

"Leander," she whispered faintly, reaching for him. "I love you, too. Leander—"

But when she opened her eyes, he wasn't there.

Twelve

He could live without her. He could live without anybody.
At least that was what he'd believed until now.

The pain without Heddy was unbearable, and Leander hadn't even endured it a week. He felt like he was losing his mind. Was she all right? Was Christina? No matter how hard he tried he couldn't stop worrying about them. He couldn't stop caring.

He had been at his desk all morning, accomplishing nothing. Usually he wrote his first drafts on a long yellow pad with a soft black pencil, skipping every other line. Usually his pencil flew like lightning—he was either writing or furiously erasing and rewriting.

Today more than a dozen crumpled yellow balls lay at his feet. He hadn't written a coherent sentence.

All he'd managed were doodles and nude sketches of Heddy. He was driving himself crazy.

But at least he was sober.

Suddenly there was a roar. And then a crash.

A tree falling? No... He didn't think so. Someone was out there.

Ivak got up and bounded to the door, barking ferociously.

"Hush!"

Ivak could not resist one final howl before settling on his haunches excitedly, his alert amber eyes glued to Leander, his intelligent gray face looking as worried as any human's.

Curious, Leander glanced at his watch as he rose and went to the window. Not that he could see anything through the frosted panes.

Ivak put a tentative paw on the doorknob, whining as Leander pulled on his parka. When he opened the door, Ivak bounded outside, disappearing into the trees.

Leander stepped out onto his porch and watched the snow swirl and listened to the eerie shivering of the trees. It was barely noon, but the snowfall had thickened. It was almost completely dark when Ivak raced back barking.

At the same moment static buzzed loudly over the radio from inside the cabin.

"Muz to Pepper. Damn it, would you come in? Over."

Ivak barked more frantically in acute disappointment as Leander went back inside. Picking up his headset, he snapped down the transmitting button. "This is Pepper. I read you. Over."

Almost instantly Muz's deep voice crackled back to him. "Did you wife make it? Over."

Leander's hands began to shake as he felt the vague beginnings of fear.

Ivak nudged the door open and trotted tensely over to the fire and whined.

"*My wife?* Not sure I read. Over."

"Heddy? Is she there yet? Over."

Leander broke into a cold sweat. "Muz what the hell are you talking about? Over."

"Your wife came in on the plane from Juneau this morning—along with those cases of cigarettes and whiskey you ordered. When I couldn't contact you by radio, I loaned her my snowmobile and gave her directions to your cabin. She kept saying it was your birthday and that it was urgent she see you. She should have been there by now. Over."

"Tell me everything! Over."

Leander was pulling on his gloves and snow gear while Muz spit out the rest of the details in between intermittent bursts of static. Then Mara got on the radio, too, assuring him not to worry about the children, that she would take care of the kids for as long as necessary.

She'd brought the kids, too?

Suddenly Leander remembered the sound he'd heard outside in his woods a few minutes before—and prayed that it was her.

Nothing mattered. Nothing in the whole world.

Except finding her.

Except telling her he loved her.

The afternoon seemed much colder than the actual temperature readings of the thermometer on his porch. An unprotected amateur couldn't survive in a blizzard like this. He considered the vastness and the danger of the island's wilderness and the smallness of a single human being. Of a woman.

The chances of a woman unfamiliar with survival training lasting long were extremely slim.

He had to find her—fast. Muz had been out of his mind to let her come.

He had been out of his mind to leave her in Texas. Especially after that last night they had shared, when she had done everything in her power to make him feel loved.

He trudged through the trees in the direction of the sound he'd heard. But it was slow going in his snowshoes.

He had been a blind stubborn fool, bent on proving what he'd always been determined to prove as a child—that he could survive without anybody.

But he couldn't. *Dear God.* Had he learned that too late? *He never prayed.*

But suddenly he felt compelled to sink to his knees in the snow. "God, *please,* let me find her."

Unaware that he was crying as he got up, he plunged through the forest toward the river, calling her name.

"Heddy!"

There was no answer—just the empty sound of his own voice echoing through the trees, and the heavy silence of the great aloneness.

Ivak raced around him in ever-widening circles, his nose in the snow. For ten long minutes, they wandered aimlessly.

The gray day was so quiet and cold, so without life or color anywhere—exactly as his life would be if he lost Heddy, if he could never kiss her again, if he could never make love to her again. If he lost her now, after all they'd been through, he would feel worse, worse even than he had in those early lost years of his childhood.

Suddenly the husky stopped and sniffed the air alertly. A ridge of fur stood up along the middle of his back as he turned to his master, howling with immense excitement. Then he dashed down to the river and began barking furiously.

Hope burst in Leander's heart.

Dear God, let it be Heddy.

Leander took off, running clumsily in his snowshoes.

First he saw the overturned snowmobile, its handlebars snagged in a leafless tree branch. Then he saw the prone figure lying perfectly still on the frozen river.

"Heddy!"

He raced toward her and then knelt, pulling her limp body into his arms.

He brushed the snow off her face. He thought her unutterably lovely. She seemed to have only fallen asleep, her thick lashes lying quietly against her pale cheeks.

Terror gripped him as he kissed her blue lips. He pulled her lifeless body into his arms, cradling her head against his chest as he lifted her gently.

"Live!" he whispered hoarsely. *Live! Because I love you more than anything on earth and I'll die if you don't!*

Her lips moved, but she made no sound.

Leander.

Was he really there this time?

Was she dead or alive?

As if in a dream she heard a dog barking.

"Go away," she whispered drowsily when a warm tongue bathed her stiff face.

"No—"

Then Leander was there.

Vaguely she was aware of the great passion in his voice when he spoke, although his voice seemed to come from far, far away. Vaguely she was aware of being lifted and carried. Of her name being said over and over as he laid her on a bed and built a roaring fire. Vaguely she was aware of sips of warm brandy being forced through her frozen lips.

"I love you," Leander said gently. "I love you."

"Why did you leave me then? Why didn't you love me?"

"Dear God." His tone was low and agonized. "Those are the same questions I used to ask my mother every time I dreamed she'd come back for me when I was a kid." Gently he placed his hands against her forehead and cheeks. "My darling, I do love you. More than anything. So much it scared me. I was angry and hurt. I hated thinking you only changed your mind because Tia gave you permission to. Maybe I just wanted to prove I didn't need anybody. I don't know. But I found out I was wrong. I can't live without you. I wouldn't have hurt you for the world. I swear I'll never leave you again."

"But can you ever forgive me?" she breathed, too weak and sleepy still to open her eyes. "I was their only child. Their last hope. Only children have a lot to live up to sometimes. Barret and Tia loved me so much. They expected so much. Too much sometimes. I felt guilty every time I disappointed them. But no more. You will always be first now, I swear."

"You believed your family, and since I didn't have a family, I ran away and played tough guy. We were both wrong. I would forgive you anything," he whispered fiercely. "Anything, Sugar."

"I never stopped loving you, Leander. Even when I doubted you. Not once during all those years even when I thought—"

"I loved you, too. And never more than when you were far away and I was all alone pretending I didn't need anybody. Nothing will ever matter to me again but you. I was too hard. You showed me you loved me that last night, and I abandoned you. If you had died in the snow, I would have died, too."

"Happy birthday," she murmured, her teeth chattering as he bundled her trembling body under the covers. "I lost your present somewhere on the ice..."

"You have given me everything that I ever dreamed of, everything that I ever wanted. Love. A daughter. A family."

"Will you stay with me this time? Will you promise never to leave me? Will you—?"

"Forever. Until we die. And after. We are star mates, remember? You are my destiny."

"You used to say all that was silly."

"I'll never say it again."

She smiled weakly as he left her just for a moment to radio Muz and Mara and tell them that he had found Heddy, but that they couldn't get back to the village until the next day. Mara reassured him again that they were having a wonderful time with the children.

When Leander came back to Heddy, she was trembling and blue with chills. He stripped off their clothes and pulled her against his body under the thick covers of his bed.

And still shivering, but warming slowly, she fell asleep against his heated length.

Hours later she awoke, the warmth of his body drawing her like a magnetic force. She felt gloriously hot. Gloriously alive. Gloriously his. And incredibly in need of his love.

"Leander—"

Her husky tone had him instantly awake.

She let her hands trail across the broad expanse of his chest, twining her fingers into the silky carpet of black hair. "Leander, I want you to make love to me."

In an instant he was fully roused.

"Are you sure, Sugar? You nearly died out there in the snow."

"I'm fine." Her eyes sparkled in the dark. A lovely tawny-pink flush tinted her cheeks. "In fact I never felt so deliciously hot and wild to—"

He bent his head over hers and crushed his lips to hers. His hands caressed her.

One kiss and she was moaning softly and breathing hard. Two and she was frantic.

"Now," she urged. "I can't wait."

Her breath stopped as he lowered his black head and placed his open mouth over her breast. His hot, moist breath burningly caressed her as his tongue teased her nipple.

She wanted him with a fierceness that shocked her.

"Now." Her voice sounded strangled. "Oh, Leander, please, now!"

He pushed her underneath him and with a violent thrust joined his body to hers.

When she gasped in pleasure, his head came up and he met her brilliant gaze. His lips fashioned her name in wonder.

"Leander. Oh, Leander," she said softly, eagerly.

Quiet tears of happiness clung to her lashes. "Don't ever run away from me again. I was so afraid I'd never see you again."

"So was I." He hesitated for a long time, savoring that first moment of sexual possession, not wanting to rush. "I can be a stubborn idiot, but I love you, Heddy."

"I know," she said, her low voice trailing away on a note of tempestuous excitement as he began to move.

Wrapping her legs around him, she drew him deeper and deeper inside her as his body surged into hers. Finally she could stand no more. All the pleasure that had been denied to her for so long burst gloriously inside her, and she cried out against his lips. He felt her joy and began to shake as the same shattering wave washed him.

They lay together, sated, in that golden afterglow of their love, knowing that finally they had come home. She had been waiting for this moment all her life.

He was as incomplete without her as she was without him. He was hers—forever.

Just as she was his.

Together they were whole.

"You are my destiny," she whispered in wonder, kissing his mouth lightly.

"Ah, Sugar," he murmured, tiredly, contentedly, burying his face in the sweet-smelling hollow of her neck. "As you are mine."

"Merry Christmas," she said. "And Happy Birthday."

They fell asleep in his warm cabin in that snowy wonderland, wrapped in each others arms and in each others love, their hearts filled with ecstasy.

Epilogue

One year later
Christmas Day

Mayflower and Ivak were prancing back and forth, barking excitedly on the verandah. Their golden eyes held both love and canine torment as they studied the human family they loved from their place of temporary exile.

Heddy's tender gaze met her husband's, and her heart leapt at the depth of emotion she read in his eyes. She would never get used to the wonder of just looking at him. He was stunning in a navy suit even though his black hair was as unruly as ever as it fell across his dark brow. Even though the Santa Claus tie Attilla had given him and insisted on tying for him was not as crisply knotted as usual.

"Should we let them in?" she whispered, indicating the two desperate dogs who whined even more pitifully when

Leander glanced their way. Ivak held up his paw as if to plead mournfully to his master.

"Faker," Leander said to the dog. And then to his wife he murmured, "No way, Sugar. I'd say we have enough chaos already."

"But—"

"I have everything I need, everything I want, right here." He pulled her into his arms and kissed her, and for the length of that lingering kiss it was as if they were the only two people in the world.

Neither of them had the slightest awareness that everybody else stopped what they were doing to watch as they kissed and clung.

"I like it when they do that," Christina said with a quiet smile.

"They do it all the time," Attilla remarked impatiently as he tossed a present into her lap.

"I like it, too," Cleo said softly, unbuckling a shoe strap and then stealthily sliding the red slipper off her heel and tucking it under the plump sofa cushions.

Tia just watched them, trying to suppress a smile as Leander gripped Heddy more tightly.

"Heddy...ah, Heddy," Leander whispered against his wife's warm throat and heavy golden hair.

"Leander...my darling Leander...I never thought I could be this happy."

"It took us a while, Sugar."

His mouth sought hers again. Only when his lips at last released hers did she come back to the golden glow of the parlor, to the sound of their two dogs barking and scratching frantically on the door again, to their children and Tia.

Heddy felt very loved as Leander hugged her closer. Attilla was dashing about again, stumbling over the litter of boxes, wrapping paper, pieces of ribbon and parts to new toys as he searched for presents with tags that had his name on them. Their new baby, James Robert, a darkly handsome miniature version of his father, squealed from his bassinet every time the big star on top of the tree blinked. Cleo and Christina sat on either side of Tia as she helped them undo the gold foil bow on Cleo's giant red package.

Yes, it had taken them a while to make a life together.

But the wait had been worth it.

The past year had been full of delights. She thought of the nights they had shared in the bed upstairs, their bodies entangled even when they slept. How wonderful it was to know that if she awoke in the dark, she would find him there. He had been with her for the birth of their son. He would be with her always.

"Happy Birthday," he murmured huskily, his voice low and intimate, for her alone.

"We said that last night," she whispered. "This is Merry Christmas."

"Yeah. Right." A crooked smile lifted the corner of his sensual mouth. "Merry Christmas it is then."

He leaned down and kissed her nose. "I love you, Heddy." Suddenly his arms came around her possessively. "I love you more than I ever thought possible."

With her hands, she framed his dark face, searching his black eyes and finding, as always, her own soul mirrored there. "I love you, too."

And, of course, after such a tender, heartfelt, soul-to-soul confession, they couldn't resist another kiss.

And once again the glory of their mouths coming together made it seem that they were the only two people in the world.

The only two people in the universe, for that matter.

Until Attilla stumbled against the bassinet and James Robert began to cry....

* * * * *

SILHOUETTE® *Desire®*

COMING NEXT MONTH

#973 WOLFE WEDDING—Joan Hohl
Big Bad Wolfe
No one ever thought January's *Man of the Month,* Cameron Wolfe, was the marrying kind. But a romantic getaway with brainy beauty Sandra Bradley suddenly had the lone wolf thinking about a Wolfe wedding!

#974 MY HOUSE OR YOURS?—Lass Small
The last thing Josephine Morris wanted was to let her infuriating ex, Chad Wilkins, permanently back into her life. Yet when he proposed they have a wild, romantic *affair,* Jo just couldn't say no....

#975 LUCAS: THE LONER—Cindy Gerard
Sons and Lovers
Lucas Caldwell knew better than to trust the sultry reporter who suddenly appeared on his ranch. But Kelsey Gates wouldn't stop until she got her story—or her man!

#976 PEACHY'S PROPOSAL—Carole Buck
Wedding Belles
Peachy Keene just wasn't going to live her life as a virgin! So she proposed a no-strings affair with dashing Luke Devereaux—and got much more than she bargained for.

#977 COWBOY'S BRIDE—Barbara McMahon
Single dad Trace Longford would do anything to make new neighbor Kalli Bonotelli sell her ranch to him. But now the rugged cowboy not only wanted her ranch—he wanted Kalli, too!

#978 SURRENDER—Metsy Hingle
Aimee Lawrence had found Mr. Right—but he insisted she sign a prenuptial agreement! Now he had to prove his feelings for her ran much deeper than lust—or there would be *no* wedding....

Three brothers...
Three proud, strong men who live—and love—by

THE CODE OF THE WEST

Meet the Tanner brothers—Robert, Luke, and
now, Noah—in Anne McAllister's

COWBOYS DON'T STAY
(December, Desire #969)

Tess Montgomery had fallen for Noah Tanner
years ago—but he left her with a broken heart *and*
a baby. Now he was back, but could he convince
her that sometimes cowboys do stay?

Only from

SILHOUETTE®

Desire

CHRISTMAS WEDDING
by Pamela Macaluso

Don't miss JUST MARRIED, a fun-filled miniseries
by Pamela Macaluso about three men with wealth, power
and looks to die for. These bad boys had everything—
except the love of a good woman.

* * *

"Will you pretend *to be my fiancée?"* Holly Bryant knew
millionaire Jesse Tyler was the most eligible bachelor
around—not that a hunk with attitude was her idea of
husband material. But then, she and Jesse weren't really
engaged, and his steamy mistletoe kisses were just part
of the charade...weren't they?

Find out in *Christmas Wedding,* book three of the
JUST MARRIED series, coming to you in December...
only from

SILHOUETTE®

Desire®

Hearts of Stone

Three strong-willed Texas siblings whose rock-hard
protective walls are about to come tumblin' down!

The Silhouette Desire miniseries by

BARBARA McCAULEY

concludes in December 1995 with
TEXAS PRIDE (Silhouette Desire #971)

Raised with a couple of overprotective brothers,
Jessica Stone *hated* to be told what to do. So when
her sexy new foreman started trying to run her life,
Jessica's pride said she had to put a stop to it. But
her heart said something *entirely* different....